Dead Men's Tales

Edited by
Melissa Black

First published in Great Britain in 2017 by
FRINGEWORKS LTD

ISBN: 978-1-909573-26-0

Copyright © 2017 Fringeworks Ltd

Cover design: Darrel Bevan

Contents

Contents_____vi

Foreword_____01

The Man Remains_____03

Aye for an Eye_____19

The Wreck of the Ebony Rose_____25

Last Entry_____33

John Gull's Tale_____43

In His Own Way_____49

Shores of Leguan Island_____57

Spectre of the Eridanus_____67

Skarett's Treasure_____81

Lips_____95

The Regular_____103

The Engine Room_____115

Buried With Treasure_____123

Dead Men's Tales' Contributors_____135

Foreword

As a boy I grew up on the pirate films of the foties and fifties. No Sunday afternoon was complete without Errol Flynn or Tyrone Power swashing their buckles on the Spanish main. But as I grew these Pirate films fell out of favour and it wasnt till many years later that I was proud to have ahand in bringing this genre back to poularity in the cinema. In fact Pirates had been a constant theme of my career as an actor. My first performance at school was in the chorus of Gilbert and Sullivan's Pirates of Penzance and my first professional engagment at the tender age of 16 was as Jim Hawkins in a stage adaptation of Treasure Island. And now I guess I will always be associated with the grizzled, rum swilling, superstitious Joshamee Gibbs, Jack Sparrow's First Mate in the Pirates of the Caribbean films.

But in literature the genre never really died. I was familiar with the aformentioned Treasure Island, and Captain Blood, right up to Tim Powers' *On Stranger Tides* upon which the fourth Pirates of the Carribean film is loosely based.

Now the genre is as healthy as ever and I am pleased to present to you a selection of Pirate themed short stories from the pens (or should I say keyboards) of some of our most talented writers. All told from the perspectives of dead Pirates, these all have such rich Piratical themes as revenge, marooning, curses, oaths, messages in bottles, ship wrecks and battles played out to a backdrop of pirates; both keen and reluctant, zombies, slaves, cannibals and a mighty Kraken.

Why Frankenstein's monster even makes an appearance.

I trust you will enjoy these tales as much as I did. They almost make me want to go back to sea again...

– Kevin McNally

The Man Remains

by Julius Horne

For my past I make no apologies, for the greater part of my life has been driven by the most righteous anger that any creature might experience. In recent months, however, I have learned to temper my moods, and to embrace the world, not as an outsider, but as a man of words.

Despite my warnings, it was the fate of the captain's doomed Northwest Passage expedition that drew me towards my life at sea. Turning back from his attempt to pass through the Arctic Ocean and into the North Pacific Ocean via the seas of the North Pole, the thickening ice blocked his return to St. Petersburg. Two weeks had separated our encounters, yet much had changed aboard His Majesty's Bark *Caurus*. The sleds had been removed and many of the crew were gone, leaving only a handful of seamen to assist their captain in his journey home.

As I hauled myself aboard the vessel it seemed empty, the rime-frosted decks abandoned and shrouded in creeping mist. As my feet connected with the deck, the first sign of life was the report of a service musket quickly followed by the crushing impact of the shot against my shoulder, knocking me backwards slightly as the leaden ball buried itself deep into my flesh.

Roaring in pain and anger, I charged across the deck towards the fading cloud of smoke that rose from behind the stack of fastened barrels that surrounded the mainmast. From beneath his oilskins, my attacker's eyes were wide and filled with fear as I closed upon him, his musket falling limply as he thrust its unfixed bayonet towards me. It caught me a glancing blow on my forearm as I swung it towards the man, impacting with the side of his head and knocking him sideways and into the open cargo hatch where his body doubtless crashed into the lower decks.

With my mood inflamed I did not hesitate to turn upon a second man, close enough for me to seize around the throat and lift clear of the deck. Like a sack of bones he sagged as I crushed his throat, tossing him limply after his companion. Three more seamen shrank away from me, their hands raised in open submission as they pleaded for mercy in a foreign tongue. Turning from them, convinced they posed no threat, I marched towards the poop deck and to the small wooden door that led into the captain's cabin.

The smell of death filled the air, despite the window being open to the elements and a layer of ice across the cabin's many surfaces. Across from me, slumped over his desk, was the ship's master, Robert Walton, a pen gripped between his dead fingers, his face pressed against his final letter.

Closing the window, I wrapped the captain's body in a blanket from his bunk, setting it aside before locking the cabin door and returning to his desk. Here, starting with his logbook, I sat down and began to read.

***

It was an hour before they knocked on the cabin door.

"Come." I was gruff. Other than the occasional case of mistaken identity I'd never been treated with politeness or civility. What I was certain of, however, was that they were only given as the price of fear. The cabin door opened and two nervous men stood on the threshold. They were a rough seaman who—despite being heavily wrapped to deal with the icy temperatures outside—was short but well-built, and a taller man dressed in clothes similar to the captain.

"We need to break out of this ice," the tall one explained. "Captain Walton was clear on the matter, but we've so few men left..."

"What do you want from me?"

"Help."

"You tried to kill me."

"Well you are rather... intimidating. It was a mistake, and without the crewmen you killed, there simply are not enough of us to return to civilisation. You though, are twice as large and powerful as any man on this ship, and you have survived alone in the cold without feeling its impact."

I grunted. It was a point well made, and if I was going to live, this ship would get us to more habitable climes much sooner than if I were to abandon them to their fate.

"I will help," I said, "but those weapons must be stowed. I'll not have another man take a pot-shot at me."

He nodded. "I'm also... the ship's surgeon. Dr. Emmanuel Clay."

"A doctor?" My temper flared at this, and the man shrunk away from me. I had no doubt that he would rather have been outside in the cold than step inside a room filled with corpses.

"Come inside and shut the door," I ordered, "and tell me what became of your ship's master."

Clay was frank with me, explaining that the ship had travelled too far into the ice before the captain chose to turn back. Within a few days the vessel was locked into the ice, and an argument ensued. The men believed the man who died in the captain's arms had been a curse upon the journey, and they had hastened to throw him onto the ice. The captain refused, insisting that he be returned to his family and be given a Christian burial. I sneered at this, and the doctor paused.

"What is his name?" he asked. "And yours?"

"I have no name," I bridled, "and I shall not speak *his*."

"No name? Are you not a Christian, sir?"

"I have read the book," I said. "At first it made some sense to me, but then the vengeful god gave way to one that has no place on this world. I did consider taking my name from it; but where I was going I had no need of a name, or an identity; there is no place for me in the Christian world. I am too much the pariah."

"You will ever be an outsider without a name," said Clay. "What did you consider?"

"Eutychus, it seemed fitting. Perhaps I shall consider it again if I am determined to live."

"Well, then you had best let me see to that wound," said the doctor. "Perhaps I can extract the shot."

I reached instinctively for my shoulder, closing a hand upon it. There was no pain now, no real sensation of anything. I told him that it was fine, that I was just grazed. Despite his concern I was sure that my anatomy—the coolness of my dead flesh, the flakes of dried skin that perpetually peeled away from it—would attract more attention than I cared for. People fear me, and until this point my life it had been spent hidden in the shadows. I urged him, instead, to continue his tale.

"The crew were divided on the matter, and the majority took to the sledges, determined to head for home over the ice. A few of us stayed, but over the next two weeks we made little progress—maybe sixty miles—and there were few rations left behind. The men who abandoned us reasoned that they needed more food to cater for their greater numbers and their harder journey. For us, we would either make it home in time or else freeze to death on the ice."

So fragile, I thought, asking after the captain and the man that he had cared for.

"The body is there." Clay pointed to a large barrel on the far side of the cabin. "The captain figured rum would be the best preservative, though I suspect that was the straw that broke the camel's back. After the others left, the captain tried to get us home, but as rations dwindled he chose to sacrifice himself for the rest of the crew."

I looked upon the captain's body with fresh eyes. He had opened up the window and allowed himself to freeze to death so that his men might get a few more meagre rations. For a moment I regretted my departure. I should have stayed while he was still alive, for this captain, whom I had considered to be a kindred spirit to *him*—I glanced towards the barrel—was in fact an honourable man whose guidance I could have sought out.

"He did his duty," said Clay, "and with your extra muscle I believe his death need not be in vain."

Honour. Duty. These had been just words to me, plucked from the holy book that helped me to learn how to read. Now, however, I was seeing human qualities that had been hidden from my sight or, as is more likely, that I had chosen not to see.

***

The journey south took nearly two months, during which time I came to understand Clay and the Russian crew. To travel aboard the *Caurus* had been a great commitment and had required a great deal of trust in their captain. By doing my part, breaking the ice by hand with hammers and picks day after day, slowly forcing the ice apart, I helped them—us—upon our way. Working alongside these men it was easy for me to pick up their language, and I soon spent much of my time alongside them, learning the true nature of camaraderie and alcohol. They were still wary of me, and had insisted on me staying away when they buried the brothers I had slain, but I felt more accepted than I ever had before. In the cargo hold, drinking rum and playing games of chance, these men and I were not so different. They were rough, poorly educated and quite ugly, bearing scars and other signs of physical hardship that perhaps helped me to fit in. Occasionally they would ask questions that I evaded, like why was my pallor so grey, or how had I come by quite so many scars? The flashes of anger in my eyes kept them from prying too hard, but as we bonded more I found that my temper was eased by the familiarity, until I could at last simply stop their questions with a smile and a calm word or two.

With the men's respect, and under the advisement of Dr. Clay, they came to call me Captain Tychus, which I accepted quickly enough. With mutual purpose I perhaps needed an identity besides that of a victim, and I set myself the task of finding safe haven with renewed vigour. Soon enough, the ice thinned enough for the *Caurus* to set its sails and press southwards again, forcing its way through a narrow and uncharted channel which, Clay assured me, would have secured Captain Walton's reputation even had he failed to find the Northwest Passage. According to some Danish charts our passage into open water—as open as it could be with so many free-floating ice mountains around us—was our entry into the Davis Straights that lie between the new dominion of Upper Canada and Old Greenland. Here we faced new challenges, and my strength and endurance were quickly called into use once more as I began to acquire the skills of the sea.

The captain's map brought us to the Whaling port of Guthaven, where we found ourselves escorted into the bay by an armed ship called the *Dorothea*. Its master, a Dane, was keen to find evidence of trading with the Greenland natives, a short stocky people called the Inuit, and demanded to see our papers. As I was living in the captain's cabin, it seemed natural for me to pass myself off as the leader of the Arctic expedition. By this time I wore a thick grizzled beard, peppered with black and brown and white and grey. The men had persuaded me that I should dye it black, and the uniform colour certainly helped to mask my distinctive features. These I further hid with a heavy coat and scarf, succeeding—with Clay's assistance—in persuading the Dane of our legitimacy. Satisfied that we weren't trading illegally, the captain joined us for a drink and we discussed our predicament with him.

"We barely have the resources to replenish our supplies," said Clay. "And with half the crew gone we're in no fit state to return home. Besides, St Petersburgh is on the wrong side of Greenland."

"We need to return to one of the British ports," said I, considering my return to Europe.

"It will be a hard journey," said the Danish captain. "To the south the Royal Navy and the colonies are heavily active. You have the British trying to enforce their power while the Thirteen States have been issuing letters of marque to their private captains, permitting them to seize and pillage British ships. With a British flag you'll be judged a prize for the privateers unless you can get yourself an escort."

"An escort will do us no good," said Clay. "We'll need to put into a colonial port if we're to have any chance of getting credit and resupplying."

The captain frowned.

"Are you set on returning to England?"

"I am," said Clay. "I promised the Cap... to carry some letters to London."

"The crew aren't so bothered," I said, speaking over Clay in an attempt to hide his slip. "They're mostly Russians, although those that were keen to return to St Petersburgh abandoned the ship some time ago."

"Yes, you seem quite relaxed about that. Mutiny on the high seas is a serious crime, and—"

"Arctic expeditions aren't like a normal journey, captain. The harsh conditions and the high likelihood of death makes men afraid."

"More afraid than they are of you, sir? You seem to be a pretty formidable commander to me."

The challenge was a dangerous one, and Clay was quick to rest his hand upon my forearm as a sign that I should not react. Seeing the flash in my eyes, the Dane backed off, clearly not wishing to test my authority.

"Perhaps you should speak to the Trading Inspector," said the captain. "I'm sure that you can come to some, ah, mutually beneficial arrangement."

With those words, the Dane returned to the *Dorothea* and we were allowed into port.

***

The captain had, mercifully, been correct. What equipment we had on board for the purposes of exploration would be of little use heading southwards, and was deemed of high value by the locals, who were happy to exchange much of our equipment for water and provisions. I allowed Clay to do the negotiating—he at least knew what he would need to return to England. The rest of the crew seemed keen to leave ship the moment we reached more temperate waters. I, meanwhile, remained aboard the ship. The fewer strangers that looked upon my face during our southward voyage, the better.

We stayed long enough to strip the ship of all we did not need, and to make our Bark look more like a Greenlander. Many of the conversions applied to the *Caurus* for Arctic exploration—the double planking on bow and waterline, the placement of fortifying oak beams to protect the ship against the external pressure of the ice, and the extra crow's nest to improve spotting from high on the main mast had already been done by Walton. All that remained for us here was to add a whaleboat or two, ring the deck with davits to sling them into the water at a moment's notice, and to stock up on the boat-hooks and grommet irons needed to harpoon and land a whale. The luxury of a cannon-fired harpoon was beyond our means, while Clay was ashore plying the Trade Inspector with Walton's rum (which for delicate reasons previously inferred was no longer to the crew's liking) the crew and I were busy learning the basics of our new trade.

I could see the appeal of such a life. My strength set me apart from the men around me, and for all its gruesome details the life of a whaler—to battle the rough seas and to pit oneself against the greatest of the Earth's beasts—seemed like a simple yet fulfilling one. I'd need a new crew—for Clay and the Russians would not stay for such a life, but the right crew can always be found for a share of the spoils, and according to men around me I was well suited to leading such a venture.

When the time came for us to leave, Dr Clay's efforts had earned us a fresh set of registration documents and letters of authority. It was not the *Caucus* that set out from Guthaven, but the *Juuls Gave*, a ship of the Royal Greenland Trading fleet.

***

By the time we reached Nantucket we had made our first kill, a hefty Greenland Black that yielded more than a dozen tons of blubber and two more of baleen. With a green crew it had been a struggle, but I was determined that the men should take some profit home with them, and we had other more experienced ships around us. I learned in those weeks that I was ideally suited not just to the life of a whaler's master, but also to the hurling of an iron.

We lost one crewman—Bogdan—a quiet but reliable man whose no nonsense outlook on life would have been a fine example for me to follow. It is strange to think that I mourned his loss—the loss of a man who saw death as a daily risk—more than the lives I had seen snuffed out against their will. With Bogdan, who had been our first line coiler, jerked into the sea by the great whale's first lunge, there had been no words. We had recovered him, still conscious, from the sea. His chest had been crushed as he had been tugged deep underwater, and as he lay there, blood and water frothing out of his mouth, there had been resignation in his eyes. Perhaps seeing that changed me, made me less angry and more understanding of the real world, not the one of privilege that *he* belonged to.

Our prize—at £40/- per ton of blubber and £400/- per ton of baleen translated into well over a thousand pounds, enough to pay off the crew and prepare for a return to the sea. With a new crew and a new outlook on the world, I embraced my life as a whaler. I had, foolishly, believed that I might end my days upon the Arctic ice, intent upon ridding the word of the cursed, soulless monster that I had become. Once death has come upon you, I realised, it cannot be easily revisited. With my vigour renewed I desired not to kill myself, but to live another life.

With Emmanuel Clay's departure I felt I was losing a friend. I had come close to telling him my story on several occasions, and I was resolved to confide in him one day—perhaps through the correspondence that we agreed to maintain. It was difficult to adjust to a new crew. Two of the Russians had chosen to stay with me, but the rest, while experienced whalers, were inexperienced when it came to dealing with their captain. The Russians kept them in line, and slowly they warmed to me as I to them, especially when we hunted the bowheads, where my strength and stamina stood me in good stead as a worthy leader and a man not to cross.

I served three seasons happy with my lot aboard the *Juuls Gave*, but whaling was not the entirety of my life. Each night I would read by the light of the oil I had hunted, working my way through the notes of the man that made me what I am, while *he*—from the rum barrel that never left my side—was kept from the peace that a proper burial might bring.

My improving literacy and my enquiring mind had led me, during my visits to port, to acquire many books associated with anatomy, biology, botany and electricity. I had had no formal education—nor could I ever hope to acquire one with an appearance such as mine—but over the months I divided my time between reading and repeating what scientific experiments I could. I dissected fish and seals, studied lenses to understand the diffraction of light, built friction generators and flew kites to capture the power of the electric storm. I developed an understanding of the different disciplines in my efforts to appreciate *his* notes. These were, as I had previously assumed, not the ravings of a madman, nor the works of someone content with privilege. They were, instead, the writings of one driven by a passion for knowledge and understanding that rivalled my own.

Had I misjudged him? No. The man had no conscience. That, I realised, was something I had been discovering in my return from the cold North. I had not just acquired an appreciation for life and its mysteries, but also for the bond between men and for the way that shared experiences created warmth and affection such as I had never felt before. My humours were, like the ice mountains of the Arctic, melting as I moved further south. But despite the camaraderie I now felt with the crew of the *Juuls Gave*, I was still driven by desire. Once it had simply been to find purpose, or to find a mate, but now it was more. Now it was the desire to be a better man than Victor Frankenstein, and to solve the mysteries he failed to understand.

There, I have committed his identity to paper, and with that, perhaps I can move forwards. It has become clear to me, as I have consumed his notations that Victor did not know *why* he had succeeded, only how. He had discovered the means to restore dead tissue to life. The key, it would seem to me, lay not with the methods of Galvani, but within the field of botany.

Bringing inanimate tissue to life is a mere parlour trick when compared to Victor's achievement. By immersing my body in a galvanic medium he was able to animate my entire body, but that could only be achieved by allowing it to heal first. But how does dead tissue heal? The answer lay in a process wherein one organism might interact with another so intimately that they become as one. He had experimented with certain forms of lichen, referencing the works of Linnaeus and Acharius, which I was able to acquire during a brief springtime sojourn among the libraries of Providence. He observed that the growth of lichen was entirely dependent upon its relationship with whatever it bonded to, and that such bonding was as possible with plants and animals as it was with rock. The properties of lichen—particularly its ability to absorb water and its known healing properties—suggested to Frankenstein that if he could find the correct lichen and suspend it in a galvanic medium such as saltwater, then as it grew, bonding with the tissue on which it was being cultivated, it might enable animation to be restored to the whole, rather than simply to the parts.

Looking down upon my own grey flesh I see the fruits of his labour. What I had taken to be dead skin created by my unique condition I now recognise as the life-giving plant upon whose existence I depend. Alas, with my new-found knowledge, I was no longer certain that whaling would satisfy me—I needed to pursue the sciences.

So it was that I employed a new ship's surgeon—Charles Gordon—a Scotsman who had come to me with a recommendation from Dr Clay, to whom I replied with thanks, asking if he could also find me a botanist. One condition of Gordon's appointment was that he should help me to learn Latin, and allow me to shadow him when carrying out his surgeon's duties. Our friendship grew—though not quite as close as the one I had come to share with Clay—and when our botanist was found, I decided that it was time for me to confess the truth to the senior members of my crew.

***

Our course had been set for warmer climes, to the south coast of the colonies. The Royal Navy had long since brought the rule of law to the high seas, with the Americans turning to whaling as a more profitable opportunity. Now, with the various wars of Independence occurring along the East Coast, there was a resurgence of the pirate and the privateer which kept many whalers away from coastal waters. There was therefore no little surprise in my decision to take us to Charleston, and as we weighed anchor I called together Grigor—the first mate, Konstantin—the boatswain, Dr Gordon and our newly appointed botanist, Thomas Lyall.

"Gentlemen," I said, "I need you to inform the crew that we are ceasing operations as a whaling ship as of this night. Any that wish to put ashore will be paid off, and the shortfall is to be made up of men with knowledge of the Caribbean and, in particular, the jungles of the south."

"*Yób tvoyú mat*," said Konstantin under his breath, clearly unhappy with my pronouncement. A brief exchange with Grigor followed, in which they discussed the merits of staying or going. They were close, and their difference of opinion was a struggle for them, but I slammed my fist onto the table to quieten them.

"I want both of you to stay with me if you will, at least until any new crew are settled."

"Captain," said Grigor, taking the initiative. "Our loyalty is not in question, and I am sure we will both stay but this—he swept his arms around the room to draw his attention to the ship—it is not the right vessel for these waters. Surely is surely better to give up the *Juuls* and its crew in favour of another."

"That is my concern too," said Konstantin, regaining his composure. "We have been with you since you came aboard and we know your fears about taking on a new crew but something smaller and better armed would suit your purposes."

"I will not change ship," I argued. "We may lack cannon, but we can acquire them, either here or in the Danish West Indies. As a whaling ship we are an unlikely target for the Colonial privateers, and I doubt the Royal Navy will give us so much as a second glance. Most whalers in these waters are passing through, and both blubber and baleen require specialist trade. Our mission shall, for the most part, be scientific."

"What is it we'll be doing in the Caribbean?" Lyall asked.

"I became master of this ship by chance, and the man that led me here still rests in the sealed barrel that sits in my quarters. His name was Victor Frankenstein, and he was a godless scientist who sought to create new life through reanimation."

"Create life? That's impossible", said Gordon. "Preposterous!"

"On the contrary, Doctor. Throughout my time aboard this ship the crew have been occupied by one question. The one question I have steadfastly refused to answer until now."

"The scars," said Grigor. "The crew has always been curious as to how you acquired so many, and why they are so regular."

I stood, removing my coat and unbuttoning my shirt, exposing my torso to others for perhaps the first time in my life. The officers stared in silence as I completed my task, and Gordon's jaw hung low in shock as the realisation dawned.

"Those are dissection scars," he said at last. "Classic cuts from lessons in anatomy. How could a living man endure such treatment?"

"I believe you have answered your own question, Doctor," I said at last. "Look also at the proportions and the subtle differences in size between this forearm—" I laid the two arms side by side "—and this."

"It can't be," said Gordon, struggling with my revelation.

"Frankenstein's notes have catalogued every component limb and organ. Its dimensions, to whom it once belonged, from where it was sourced. I am a patchwork resurrection, gentlemen. A whole human being reconstructed from the offcuts of the dead."

The silence was palpable. Konstantin crossed himself, but he and Grigor kept their places. We had perhaps been together too long for them to doubt me, and also—I hoped—to reject me. Gordon seemed uneasy, his mind doubtless recoiling from the impossibility of my words, but Lyall had leaned forwards, intense fascination upon his face.

"As a botanist I am, perhaps, more open to the idea of wholesale transplantation, but are you saying that *every* part of your body was once dead?"

"According to Victor's notes," yes. "I had not considered that some part of me may have clung to life—perhaps because it would violate my creator's philosophy. There is yet more proof; the purpose of our expedition to the jungles of the south.

"Here," I said, thrusting my wrist towards Lyall. "The flakes of skin that crumble as you touch them. What are they?"

Lyall leaned in, scrutinising my pallid flesh as none since Victor Frankenstein himself had done. After a moment, he reached into his pocket and withdrew a hand lens, following the granular pattern of the thin crust that covered my body from head to toe. As he did so, realization dawned upon his face, and the lens was lowered as he made his pronouncement.

"It is a lichen thallus," he said, "and it is growing between the pores of your flesh."

"The lichen continues to grow, feeding on my body just as it once enabled me to feed upon the life-giving electricity that Victor used to precipitate the healing process. This is how he restored a patchwork corpse to life. That lichen will be the key to reproducing his life's work."

"Reproducing?" asked Gordon. "Sir, while I respect your desire to understand the process, this Frankenstein's work is an abomination. It should not be repeated."

"Come, Dr Gordon," said the botanist, "if this lichen can be combined with an electrical charge to restore life to dead tissue it represents the *transference* of life from plant to animal. It is not the *creation* of life, merely the restoration of its function resulting from a shared biology."

"And who would volunteer to be restored in such a fashion? Do you retain the mind of the man or woman whose brain was acquired for this experiment?"

"I believe not," I said, shaking my head. "I have no memory before I awakened, although I am curious as to whether or not such things might be reawakened."

"Then you are nothing but a walking corpse."

The words enraged me, and for the second time that evening I hammered the table. This time I exercised such force as to splinter it beneath my fists, sending food and wine crashing to the floor as I roared in anger. The others scattered, drawing back from me in fear that my rage might become physical violence.

"*I have memories now, doctor!*" I screamed. "Be sure to remember that before you speak so offensively."

"I... I... apologise, captain," he said at last. "You must understand that reconciling my beliefs with the principles of my profession can be difficult. I mean only to say that if no memory is retained, then why would any man wish to be healed in this fashion. Who would volunteer for such an experience?"

"One man would," I replied. "The one man who dared to question, and who lost his life by embracing the consequences of his terrible actions. *That* man!"

I pointed towards the sealed barrel, wherein Victor Frankenstein's pickled corpse resided.

"Mr Lyall," I said, desperately attempting to regain my composure, "his notes include the study and indexing of various lichen which include the sample used when I was revived. I no longer have access to those, but the taxonomy of the lichen is carefully detailed, and that particular sample was found growing on an underwater rock in the jungles of the Darién south of Panama.

"My plan is simple. Mr Lyall and I shall recover as much of the lichen as we can find. Then it is my hope that you, Dr Gordon, will assist me in replicating Frankenstein's work. I intend to bring my creator back to life. Only then will we know if a man can be restored in both mind and body, and whether or not my own loss of memory is a result of the dissection."

"Captain," said Grigor, "we cannot share this with the men. I am not even sure you should have shared it with us. If even one of the men in this room chooses to leave..."

He left his conclusion unspoken, but he was right. Any man that walked away from this would have to be silenced. Permanently. I cursed at the thought. I was becoming what I despised, protecting my intentions at all costs, with no consideration of the consequences for others.

"Very well," I said. "It is time for you to decide if you wish to stay or go. Any among you that leaves us now must stay silent. Forever. For if I learn that you have spoken of this matter to anyone I shall come, I shall find you, and I shall kill you."

"Captain," it was Lyall that spoke first, "it would be an honour for me to stay with you and to share in the discovery that lies ahead. I cannot think of a more significant goal."

"I too shall stay," said Grigor. "We have come too far together, and to understand the pain you have endured, I cannot abandon my friend. Konstantin?"

The boatswain grunted his agreement. Whether out of friendship or duty, he was setting aside his initial objections and I knew, in my heart, that he would remain loyal. This left only the ship's surgeon to state his position.

"I suppose," said the doctor, "that Thomas is correct. My objections are hypothetical. Until the proper observations have been made I cannot pronounce on the ethics of the matter. I reserve the opportunity to state my case when those observations are made, and I insist upon making a thorough investigation of your physiognomy. At the very least I can independently verify or disavow Dr Frankenstein's work."

"Then the matter is settled," said I. "Make the arrangements, Grigor, and I shall join you ashore in the morning. If I am to be seen as Captain I shall make the effort and dress formally. We need to make a good impression if we are to find new crew."

***

FROM THE SOUTH-CAROLINA GAZETTE, 7 MAY 17—

The arrival of a Bark flying Danish colors on the 27th of April last aroused unrest among the locals who viewed its nocturnal appearance— accompanied by the glow of spirit candles resembling the fires of St Elmo—as a bad omen.

The Barks company took up at Shepheard's Tavern in search of new crew, but a disturbance followed when the ships master, E Tychus, entered. Based upon the man's height and demeanour, and upon the appearance of a decapitation scar across his throat, patrons believed the man to be none other than the notorious pirate Edward Tache who died in the Pamlico Sound over eighty years since.

Captain Tychus killed several locals and obliged the remainder to quit the tavern. By the time the city militia were alerted Tychus and his crew had got away into their boats along with at least three Negro runaways who are thought to have assisted them in their escape. A considerable number of Negroes came off afterwards in canoes and departed aboard the Bark whose name was not recorded.

The intendant's office has confirmed that a formal approach will be made to the Chamber of Customs on the Island of St Thomas.

Aye for an Eye
by Patrick O'Neill

Judge Hadley,

Surprised to hear from me? I'll bet you are.

The last time our eyes met I was swinging from the noose—dancing the hempen—and how I swung. Quite an event, wasn't it? Nice turnout. I was flattered by the gibbet cage too. I know you only save that for the worst of us—or the best—depending on which side of the law you fall.

And I am the best, which is why you took so long to catch me, and why I still found a way out. The best pirates always do.

When Old Barnsey kicked away the chair and I heard my neck go, I smiled at you, remember? And you laughed back at me with that stupid, arrogant look on your face, bathing in victory.

I've been a merciless thief and a ruthless liar, but I never killed a man. The worst I ever did was cut out that Navy boy's eyes and tongue. The fish took care of the rest. He should have surrendered the boat while he had the chance. Shame he turned out to be a Judge's son, but all the same, that's what you get when you cross Slicer Stokes. I never forget, and the fish knife is always close at hand, ready for the bloody work.

Maybe you heard what happened to Old Barnsey last week. They say when they found him in his bed he was wearing the executioner's mask. And when they took it off, they saw his eyes had been gouged out, and his tongue cut off.

Who's laughing now, Judge?

Strange feeling when you hang. Breath gets strangled out of your lungs and you can't get it back. Blood stops pumping and grows cold. Then it sinks down to your feet and makes them bloat like bags of water.

Even as the life drained out of me, I kept smiling because I knew I'd settle our score in the end.

Through the rusty bars of the gibbet cage, I saw you all on the beach, as before, but now painted in vivid crimson and magenta, deep emerald and gleaming gold. The sea was a dark mass, rolling and gently swaying. Clouds stretched the length of the cove like white tentacles against the blood-red skies. Life through a dead man's eyes.

"I'll see you in Hell, Stokes," you called out.

And as I hung, heavy and limp, creaking in the wind, I thought: *No, I'll see you before then, Judge.*

When you came towards me across the sand and ordered Old Barnsey to lower the gibbet, I knew exactly what you were going to do even before you unsheathed your knife and reached inside the cage. An eye for an eye; a tongue for a tongue. Right Judge?

You didn't get it quite right though. Not on the left eye. Not like I got it right with your boy. He had nothing but gaping holes when I was done. But I still see everything.

I remember how he screamed in the bloodstained water by the side of the ship, scratching blindly at the wood of the hull, knowing the sharks circled beneath. He tried to speak, but it wasn't all that easy with a mouth full of blood.

Still, I wouldn't expect an educated man to be handy with a knife. You shook and that never makes for the best cuts. You have to relax and let the blade do the work. It's not something you can learn overnight. Gutting a fish is easy but when you're working on a living man, it's a different matter. A test of the nerves and the stomach.

I wonder if you smelt me when I pushed this letter under the door of your chambers only five minutes ago. I'll bet you did. Flesh rots slowly, but the stench gets richer and deeper as the days pass.

As the gibbet swung across the waves and lowered into the ocean, I watched you smile in that smug, triumphant way. Your hands and wig drenched in my blood. Icy salt water gushed through the bars and into my severed eyes. The screaming gulls became silent as my senses filled with the roar and suck of the ocean around me. Amongst the seaweed, fish swarmed about my face, tearing chunks from my lips and wriggling through my beard to seek out the soft flesh beneath.

Some of them went for my feet, which were swollen and heavy with blood. As their little teeth punctured my skin, pressure released and I knew it was only a matter of time before the water became red and bigger fish would arrive.

A small squid slithered and sucked its way across my face, clenching its tentacles about my neck, and then, ahead of me, a large shadow passed, making the cage sway against the current. Then another, close enough this time to see the smooth grey and white skin and the razor teeth. For a moment, I panicked, but then I remembered all would be well.

Let me explain, your Honour.

The first time I met him was in a smoke-filled bar in Brente, a small harbour town of just south of Calais. He sat in a darkened corner, hidden beneath a black hat, with a walking stick propped against the fireside.

He was an old man, frail and alone. Easy pickings.

The gold coin twisted through his fingers and caught my eye. He seemed to be talking to himself, but it was hard to tell. His face was half-obscured as he stared into the flames. The other drinkers huddled about the bar, out of earshot, and so I approached him.

As I neared, he ushered a thin hand to the chair beside him, as though sensing my arrival.

I lifted the tricorn from my head, rested it on the table between us, and sat by the fire. The flames rose and licked around the logs, creaking and hissing into the silence, but no warmth there, only a terrible coldness that ran through to the bone.

I glanced again at the gold coin twisting and flipping easily through his slender fingers.

"See something you like, Stokes?" he asked.

He held his gaze on the fire, and I saw that his eyes were blacker than night. Flames danced in their darkness.

"Stokes isn't my name, old man."

A thin smile crept about the corners of his mouth as he continued to stare at the fire.

"Games are for the weak, Stokes. Maybe I was wrong about you after all."

"If you think I'm Stokes, you'll know not to play with me. Things can change quickly when foul tongues speak. I could have you spitting teeth with your face pressed against the fire in a second."

"As I said, games are for the weak."

He flipped the gold piece up, and I caught it mid-flight. When I opened my palm, the coin was no longer gold, but the green colour of old copper.

"Now who's playing games?" I said.

He turned to me and my blood ran cold as I saw his face properly for the first time in the flickering light.

"I have an offer for you, Stokes. Listen."

And so it came to be, Judge.

It's not all about taking when you're a pirate. Sometimes you need to give a little too, if the offer's right, and this time it was. No doubt. I knew your men were closing in. You can run for so long and I had gotten tired and needed some kind of security, and The Master offered it in bounds.

A simple contract between gentlemen, irreversible and written in blood: life beyond death in return for a stake in my soul. The Master was true to his word, as I knew he would be.

Here I am, good as new. Well, almost. Let's just say I'm not quite the man I once was and leave it there.

I'd like to have seen your face when you pulled the gibbet up from the depths, rusty and dredged in rotten seaweed, but most definitely empty. What did you think? That the fish had left nothing? Poetry, isn't it? The perfect result. I become legend, and you become the judge who thought he'd hung Slicer Stokes. What a fool you are.

I'll admit, it's not easy for me now. I'm not used to taking orders from anyone. I've never played fiddle for any man in all my working life, and I've never been called to task. Anyone who attempted to dominate was sliced aside. But a deal is a deal, and the Master tells me there will be rewards, and I know he means business.

Old Barnsey was the first port of call. Being around death so much, I expected him to have a little more in the bottle, but he kicked and squealed like a hog under the blade. In the end, I pulled the mask down over his head and made him drown by his own bloody mouth just to stop the noise. That's justice.

Afterwards, The Master mentioned Elizabeth to me. Well, that was news. I never knew you had a daughter. I couldn't

help laughing when I found out though. You kept that one quiet didn't you, Judge? I heard she was to be married in the spring. Virgin bride, eh?

She was tending the horses in the barn when I found her. You should have seen the look on her face when I walked in.

Once her eyes were out, the real fun began. Pretty, wasn't she? Tight as an anchor's knot too. Once I was done, I strung her up by her feet and cut off her ears. She didn't like that too much, Judge. Don't worry though, I didn't make it last too long. There's only so much complaining I can take. In the end, I bled her into a metal bucket until she stopped flinching. She was paler than the moon by the time I finished.

You must have wondered where she'd gotten to these last few days. I'll bet you did. Try the gibbet down on the cove. I put it back under the surface. Best sea burial I could think of. The fish will have gotten to her properly by now. Ocean's bride. Not so pretty and tight after all.

Like I told you, don't cross the Slicer.

You can you smell me now, can't you? I'm right behind you as you read. I am here for the Sentencing.

I brought The Master with me this time. He likes to watch. Just wait until you see his face; his eyes. One Hell of a sight, let me tell you.

I'll just cut out one eye to begin with, because we're taking the fun down to the cove. It'll be dark but the moon is full tonight. I wanted to give you a chance to see what we've

done to Elizabeth before I take the other eye, and you swap places with her. Look on the bright side: at least you get to see your family.

But what a way to end it. Who would have thought? Judge Hanger Hadley himself, dangling there against the tide and the full moon. No eyes, no hope, no tongue, no kids.

You could try and make a deal with The Master, but I reckon it's a little late in the day for that. Besides, I don't think you have the stomach for this kind of work. It takes a certain type to see these things through. And what use is a shaking hand?

Now, are you ready? It's getting on, and there's no time to waste.

So go on, turn around and take look at your handiwork. Take a look at what the fish did to me. Take a look at your justice. Take a look at your fate. Meet The Master.

I've got my fish knife so you better hold still. Don't be like Old Barnsey. Take it like a Judge.

The Wreck of the Ebony Rose

by Rie Sheridan Rose

An inch of pencil stub and two of candle…perhaps I shall finish my tale, perhaps not. Is it enough to try? You shall judge.

My name is—was—Abraham Colter. I went to sea as a lad of ten, running off from a drunken father and a mother too burdened with other brats to notice one missing. I had first seen the tall sails when I was but a toddling whelp of three, and I fell instantly beneath the spell of salt and spray. As soon as I could coil a rope and scale a mast, I was off and never once looked back.

Of course, as a landlubber with naught but the shirt on my back and a yen for the sea, I was ripe for sorrow. Luck favored me—whether for good or ill is a question for sharper heads than mine—when I was taken aboard the Ebony Rose to sail as her cabin boy.

The captain, a darkly handsome devil of a pirate by the name of Tobias McCann, had taken quite a fancy to my eagerness, and painted a picture of adventure that was irresistible to a sea-struck child.It seemed a dream come true. A sovereign per journey, food and bunk, a share of looted treasure, and the skill to find a mate's berth one day if I paid heed to my duties and was quick to learn. The glamour of a pirate's life—a boy's fantasy made real. So I took the crown he offered and made my mark, feeling ten feet tall instead of ten years green. I sailed beneath that jolly flag for the next dozen years. And then, we met the wreckers.

***

The moon hid behind a mask of tattered clouds, the night sodden with the threat of rain. Surf pounded an angry tattoo against the jagged rocks at the foot of Deadman's Cliff as the wind keened in wailing counterpoint. The briny dark flared with the sudden sharp scent of flint striking tinder, and pitch snapped as a huge lantern ignited into blinding light. Reflectors caught the flame and magnified it a thousand fold, illuminating the hard rugged faces of desperate men. A dozen circled the lantern, making last checks of equipment as the light steadied into a strong beam. Low voices muttered like the surf.

A second lantern beam joined the first. The lights were fastened to the panniers of a blinkered donkey that fidgeted at the end of a tether, made restless by the storm.

"This is my last go, Ryan."

"Leave off that talk, O'Connor. You're in just as deep as the rest."

Seamus O'Connor fumbled with the brim of his slouch hat. "I'm leaving here in the morning, Ryan. Going inland to work in the brickyard with Moira's da. I can't take this no more."

A stubby finger, hard as iron, poked the center of O'Connor's chest. "Let's see you try, bucko. You know as well as I that leaving here isn't as simple as deciding to run." Ryan cuffed O'Connor lightly on the jaw. "We'll see what you say when all is said and done. That lovely young bride of yours needs pretty things and that takes money you'll never see at no brickyard."

O'Connor saw Moira's trusting face in his mind's eye, and bowed his head. Ryan was right. She deserved a better life than he could offer her as a fisherman or a bricklayer. He couldn't leave the life, no matter how much he hated it. The ships brought liquid gold in their holds—brandy and rum, fine wines from Spain and France. Silks from the Orient. Spices with their heady perfumes. A man could earn a fortune overnight with the luck behind him.

Rain spat from the heavens as if showing its contempt for the business at hand. The wind howled maniacally. Ryan slapped O'Connor on the back.

"Come on, boyo. Start the donkey on its way. The sea will be good to us tonight. I can feel it."

Sighing defeat, O'Connor swatted the donkey with a flick of a hickory switch. A bray of token protest, and the animal plodded forward along the edge of the cliff. Ryan and his band of wreckers swarmed down the slick rocks toward the narrow bar of sand behind the jagged teeth below. They hid themselves among the shadows, weapons at the ready.

***

The Ebony Rose rode the surging swells like a silent queen, her sails glowing ghostly in the dim moonlight. Even the creaking ropes were eerily muffled in the growing fog as she sailed on. Dark as midnight shone the wet wood of her planks. The Roger snapped in the wind above the crow's nest, but it too was silent.

Our crew spoke no word as they moved about their stations. Tonight, after a long and weary voyage, the ship would reach our home port at last. Her hold was full of stolen treasure, but it had been hard won. Half a dozen hands would not be greeting loved ones tonight. Standing at the wheel in his blood-red coat, Captain McCann searched the horizon for his first sight of shore. He always did so—every time we neared this port.

I had worked my way up to his right hand in our dozen years together—from cabin boy to mate—and I knew what he was searching for, there in the darkness…her candle in the window—Joanna calling him home.

A lantern hung from the bowsprit, lighting the figurehead gracing the prow of the ship. The carving was magnificent, intricately detailed, a delicately beautiful woman with a white dress and flowing black hair. The ebony rose that gave the ship her name was clutched in one ivory hand. She pointed to sea with the other hand, bare feet poised as if to step forward into the surging waters. The master woodcarver had given her an expression of utter longing. It personified the ship and was a portrait of Tobias's wife.

***

O'Connor walked the donkey slowly along the headland, back and forth along an arc of coast, the lanterns flickering wildly in the rising gale, but holding their own. He had no stomach for this work anymore. He had lived in Braeden's Head all his life. He remembered wading for flotsam in the icy surf when he was five.

His da was a wrecker, and his before him. Fishing to eat, but making their true living from the bounty of the ships, and to hell with the sailors who went to their graves because of it.

A memory flashed through his thoughts. He had been no more than eight and fell asleep on a pillow of sand, waiting with the wreckers for a ship to take the lanterns' bait. When, the night shattered around him as the rocks claimed another victim.

There was an initial thunderous crash as the prow of the ship hit the first jagged boulder, and then the eerie groaning screeches of the planks as they splintered and broke beneath the onslaught.

It was his first time at the wreck itself—before he had only seen the aftermath. The ship had been a passenger ship. A few of the men and women were better swimmers than others. A handful made it to shore. He watched the wreckers bludgeon them to death with clubs and rocks to make sure there were no survivors to tell the tale.

He had been sick in the bloodied water.

But it had hardened him too. Though he had volunteered to man the lanterns from that day forth, and never participated in the blood work, as if that somehow kept his hands clean. The attempt to break with Ryan tonight had been a half-hearted gamble at best. He didn't want to stay in this life, but there was no way out as long as Ryan knew his name.

He scanned the horizon—sails upon the sea, making for shore. Time to go to work.

***

When I was a boy, my best friend was Seamus O'Connor. His da and mine were drinking mates. He was a mite younger than me, but I enjoyed his company. Sometimes he bought me sweets. He seemed always to have coins, while I never did.

When I left to sea, we seldom saw each other anymore. Sometimes, when the Rose made port I would stand a pint at the pub, but last trip home I heard he had married the McBride girl. That would no doubt put an end to our carousing. I wished him well, but the sea was the only wife I wanted.

As we surged toward port, I considered whether I should look Seamus up. We'd been to sea for over a year, after all. Sometimes one longs for companions who know your secrets. I wasn't that close with the crew. I searched the shoreline with Tobias, eager to be home, even if there was no Joanna awaiting me. I didn't see the prick of candlelight in the fog, but I did see the guide lights.

"There, Toby! There's the light house. We'll be home within the hour." I clapped him on the shoulder. I'd buy you a pint, if I thought you'd take it."

"Joanna will be waiting, Abe. You know that." His voice was soft, but with a lilt she always brought to his mood, an eagerness to be home with her. To kiss the babe she'd been expecting when we put to sea.

I shook my head with a fond chuckle. She was the only thing on his mind, as usual. Still, he was a good master, and I was happy to serve under him, pirate or not. I glanced up at the shoreline again and frowned. Something was wrong. "Tobias—"

The Rose hit the outlying rocks with a screech of tortured wood and screaming metal. It was so quick that the hands below never had a chance. Those of us on deck were flung from our feet. Several careened over the rail with cries of pain and terror.

Tobias clung to the wheel, his face ashen in the flickers of moonlight—so close to Joanna and yet so far from home. He fought to hold course. If he could maneuver the Rose just a bit closer to shore, some of us might make it ashore alive. He was determined to save anyone he could. But it was too late.

The ship listed badly, taking in water by the moment. I could see the rocks now, glowing with foam—sharp teeth biting into the Rose like a hungry shark.

"How did we lose our way, Abraham? This harbor is our home. We were both born and raised here."

"Wreckers," I growled—pointing to the lights. They were moving along the headland. I should have seen before, but I was just as eager as Tobias to be home.

"They've taken my ship, but they will not take me easy," the captain cried, drawing the brace of pistols from his belt and brandishing them at the rocks.

I drew my own cutlass, ready to go down at his side.

The tilt of the deck made it difficult to keep our feet. Tobias and I fought to reach the prow and the lantern hanging there.

He gave a heart-wrenching groan when he saw the figurehead had been split in two. The loss of Joanna's likeness was the final crushing blow to his spirit. He fired blindly across the waves.

"Save your bullets, man," I chided, grabbing at his arm. "There will be a dozen men at least. For all I know we two are all who survive on the Rose."

The storm had broken in earnest now. The wind howled like a demon and rain lashed us like whips, the deck slick and treacherous beneath my boots.

And then the ship gave a mighty lurch, throwing me over the rail and into the boiling sea. My head slammed into a rock, and I sank beneath the water.

I fought to regain the surface, trying to kick off my boots, desperate to survive. My head broke the surface, and I gasped for air. Some miracle had left me my cutlass, and I stared about me in the uneven light, disoriented as to where the shore lay.

I struck out where I hoped to find rescue. I felt the crunch of sandy gravel beneath my feet and staggered to the shore. Thanking a benevolent God, I fell to my knees, retching seawater.

But God must be capricious.

I heard the crunch of boots upon the sand and rose to my feet, cutlass clutched in shaking hand. My vision blurred and doubled, blood running into my left eye, diluted by rain and sea. The wreckers had found me. They circled like rats—men I knew, had grown up with, toasted in the pub. And there was Seamus O'Connor, who once had been my friend.

***

Seamus thought he had waited long enough before he ventured down the cliff. The ship listed hard, the cries of the dying silenced. But he was wrong.

He reached the shore and pulled the shillelagh from his belt. Cargo bobbed among the surf, already beginning to drift ashore, and he could see it would be a rich haul. He reached for a crate, dragging it to the sand.

As he reached for another, a beam of moonlight hit the tattered flag snapping in the howling wind. His blood ran cold. It was the Jolly Roger. His gaze searched the wreck and found the ruined figurehead. He knew this ship.

"Bloody hell, Ryan. What have we done?"

He ran to the circle of wreckers gathering on the sand. There was a sailor in their midst, trying to keep them at bay with shaking sword. No, not a sailor—a pirate. One of Tobias McCann's if he was right about the ship. And then he saw the man's face. A face he recognized. A face he'd never thought to see at the other end of a wrecking run.

"Seamus," whispered the pirate.

His hand came up instinctively, bringing down the shillelagh with a resounding crack upon the other's head.

***

I saw the club in his hand, saw him raise it against me, and then the world went black as he brought the weapon down upon my skull. I floated free of my crumpled corpse, but I needed to tell the tale. Joanna deserved to know how Tobias loved her more than life itself.

I suppose my candle and pencil stub were enough after all. My story is done. I'll leave this journal here in the captain's cabin. It's still above the water, and I trust that the wreckers will be sure to loot it before she sinks.

The Ebony Rose was a rich prize. I cannot blame the wreckers for taking her. But they've unleashed a world of pain upon this town. And now the reason will be plain. Tobias McCann will have his revenge. They say dead men tell no tales, but I suppose sometimes they are wrong.

Last Entry

by Max Wright

July 18, 1724 (by my reckoning)

*This is the log of the Free Ship Peril, formerly the sloop-of-war HMS
Peregrine. It is somewhat extraordinary, I'll warrant, to find a ship
of the Brotherhood, maintaining such a record and we have not seen
fit to do so until now, with the hopes that whoever may find this book
will offer up prayers for our wicked souls that we may be forgiven
and...*

The door to my quarters opened, the visitor unannounced by any
knock. As there was only one man aboard besides myself who was
able to make his way about the ship, I knew exactly who it was. Old
Moses, a half-civilized African whom we'd pulled off a cargo vessel near
Hispaniola a year ago. I'd taken him to be my personal servant, a position
he was accustomed having served in such employment aboard various
ships since his youth.

"What is it?" I detested being interrupted.

"Another man down, Captain." He took a step backward, as though
he expected me to dismiss him with a curt order.

We'd been blown off-course nearly a month ago, and all but becalmed
since then. Having been on the return leg of our journey, we were already
short of fresh water and victuals when the storm hit. Weakened by
hunger, the men succumbed to a vicious fever. Of our original crew of
37, some dozen had already died. This man would be the thirteenth of
our crew that Moses and I had committed to Davey Jones. I myself had

survived this long only because I kept myself on more generous rations—the captain of a vessel must always have the clearest head, and besides, rank has its privileges. Moses credited the leather pouch he wore about his neck. A *gris-gris* he called in his savage tongue and claimed it had powers to protect him from demons, disease, and even the bullets of a white man.

I stood up. "All right, then. I'll help you dispose of him." Moses did a half bow and backed out of the cabin. I followed him.

I retched as we first stepped below deck, doing my damndest not to throw up. Adding the stench of my own vomit to the horrific blend of puke, offal, decaying flesh and corruption that clogged my nose and mouth would be bad enough. Embarrassing myself would be even worse

A few of the men muttered, whether greetings or imprecations at the perceived incompetence of my command I could not say. I followed Moses to where the dead man lay in a filthy hammock spotted with his bodily waste and blood. Disposing of it was efficient; simply cut the strings suspending the hammock, fold it over (using the ends of the rope to avoid contacting the filthy thing), then haul it up the stairs and onto the deck. There Moses, who fancied himself a holy man, would mutter a few prayers as he sewed the hammock shut. Then we tossed it over the rail.As we slipped the man over the side, it seemed to me that going on like this would be fruitless with no longer enough rations to make even a pretence of feeding the sick, and it was all I could do to keep myself alive.

On the deck, the stench from the hold leaked up and spoiled a moonlit evening on still seas, I spoke to the savage.

"If we stay, we are sure to end up like those poor bastards down there."

"Yessir, Captain."

"I suggest we make our getaway. If we abandon the larger ship, we can escape aboard the boat. With two of us to man the oars and laden with what water and foodstuffs as we have, the two of us might be able to make land fall somewhere." I hated to let the black in on my plan to abandon my crew, but there was no one else to assist me, and it would take both of us to man the small boat. Besides, once we reached land, I had a brace of pistols tucked into my sash, and he did not.

"That'd be hard on them we leave behind." He looked at the moon and smiled—the look of a man who has either been inspired or gone mad. In our desperate straits, both were possible.

"Look, even if by some miracle every one of them was able to get up to and on deck tomorrow, we've barely enough left for a skeleton crew. And I don't see how that's going to happen, not unless God himself steps down onto our for'castle this minute."

Moses turned, his white teeth glinting with moonlight against his black face. "Maybe those men below, maybe we're not done with them yet. Maybe, Captain, this boat, she doesn't need such a big crew after all."

"No crew? It takes at least 10 men to man this ship and . . . My God, man, you're not suggesting that we eat — I'd heard stories of crews, driven to desperation, doing just that with their dead in order to survive, and on the last trip down below decks, there seemed to be more men missing than should have been by Moses' count. There were limits even to my unnatural inclinations.

"No sir, Captain. Eating those poor souls below won't do us any good at all. Keep us alive for a while, maybe, but without a crew, even if a breeze came up tomorrow, we couldn't sail this ship. We'd just have to hope some ship spotted us."

"And any ship that spotted us would take us in as pirates to be hanged. Hardly worth the effort of saving us." I felt in my pocket for a pipe, the one solitary joy I still had, as our holds were crammed with tobacco, taken off a Spanish ship headed out of Cuba.

"You predict my line of thought most admirably, Captain."

He bowed in a mocking way, cackling. Such disrespect probably would have earned him a good flogging on his old ship, but the Brotherhood has never been much for standing on form. If you want to spend the rest of your life *yessirring* and *nosirring*, then you might as well remain in His Majesties service and have your three squares as well.

"What do you propose?" Even as I spoke, I felt my hair begin to move about me. "A breeze, by God! " I felt my heart soar, then fall back to earth. What good would a breeze do us now? Maybe a week ago, even three or four days, we might have been able to get enough fellows up from below to get ourselves underway, but now, it wasn't going to happen.

"It's a proper breeze, Captain. Good and proper. And it's not too late, not if I can do anything about it."

At that point, I didn't care what that African bastard intended to do—I was not going to die, not now, not after enduring so much.

"Do whatever you must, but do it quickly. Who knows how long this wind will last?"

"By your order, Captain, but it would be best if you were to keep to your cabin for a day or so." His tone was menacing and insolent.

"You think it best? Free men we may be, but I'm still captain of this vessel, and there's a limit to —" I stopped. If he could truly save us, I'd owe him my life and more besides. "All right. A day in my cabin. I'll work on the log. In case your plan doesn't work as well as we hope."

He looked at me from his hollowed out, sunken eyes, and his cracked lips pulled back from around his bloody stumps of teeth. "Oh, don't you worry, Captain. My plan will work out just fine."

***

The smell from below decks has become almost unbearable. The odor of corrupting flesh is horrible enough, and now Moses' concoctions adds its own fetid stench on top of that, creating a dissonant aroma that makes the eyes water and causes bile and other poisons to rise up in the throat. I have no idea how the men below can stand it. Or what Moses is up to.

I put down my quill. Something was going on below decks—movement and I could have sworn I heard a guttural moan, like the last gasp of someone in too great a pain to cry out. Whatever Moses was up to, it wasn't working. I would have to help him dispose of the body.

I stepped out from my cabin. The sky was dark, but the breeze still blew. I made my way to the hatch and opened it. A wave of heat and the foulest stench imaginable rolled up at me. I gagged and coughed. Moses appeared below me wreathed in ghastly fumes, staring up from the depths, like the embodiment of some malign African spirit. Behind him, something made a noise and a shadow flickered in front of the firelight, as though one of the crew had moved behind him.

"What's that? Has your medicine gotten someone up and able? I can scarce imagine a man able to stomach such an obnoxious concoction as —"

Moses came up the steps towards me, pulling a dagger from his belt and pointing it at me.

"Have you gone mad? I'm still the captain . "

"That you are, Captain. And before long, I may well have need of you, but not right now. I'm in charge, at least until I have the rest of the crew up and moving again. Now, sir, I suggest you go to your cabin, and turn over your key to me."

"The rest of the crew?" The good news caused me to temporarily overlook his insubordination. "You mean you have got at least one man up and well? " I took a step down the ladder. "McGreevy? Quint? John Longshanks?" These men had been among the last of the crew to take sick, and all had been at least able to speak coherently when I'd last laid eyes on them.

Moses jabbed at my chest with the tip of the dagger. "Not another step, Captain. Be so good as to go back up the stairs and give me your key."

I took one look into his eyes. Something had changed, something deep within his very soul. I've looked into the eyes of a hundred men intent on killing me and never before known such fear as I knew then. I reached into my pocket and produced the heavy skeleton key. He took it and roughly steered me back to my cabin.

"I'll be seeing you before long now, Captain. Keep your spirits up, and you'll see the rum dives and cathouses of New Providence again."

With a fierce shove he propelled me into the room. The door slammed behind me, and locked clicked. I heard a scraping, like a cask or something being dragged across the planks of the deck. An animal cry rent the air, a harsh, inhuman noise that sent icicles into my belly and made my heart pound like the drummer on a Turkish prison galley.

Now was the time to act, I realized and hurled my shoulder against the door. It shuddered, but did not give. I tried again, throwing myself at so violently that I felt such pain as I had never before known shoot through me.

"The old *Peril*, she's a stout ship, is she not?" Moses mocked me, his laughter nearly muffled by the heavy oak of the wall and door. A series of cracks echoed in my head. They were nailing something across my door.

"Let me out, you damnable bastard!" I shouted through the keyhole, through which no light now entered.

"All in good time, Captain." His voice was faint but discernable. "You're days of sailing aren't over yet, and soon we'll have such a crew as has never been seen on any of the high seas. Mark my words, Captain, this ship is about to become the most infamous afloat."

I walked away from the door and took a seat behind my table. I had little enough faith in Moses' promise to spare my life. It was then that I recalled the ship's log, sitting untouched for days on a corner of the desk. I knew Old Moses was illiterate, so I opened the book and began to write. Someday, the log might find its way into somebody's hands. If found by the authorities, well then, it would prevent Moses from making any claims of being taken as a prisoner or held as a slave and forced to participate in piratical acts. Should the book be discovered by a member of the Brotherhood, well, while we're not so formal about things as the Royal Navy and do allow every freebooter among us a certain amount of latitude, even our most independent types take a dim view of mutiny, pure and simple. Pirate vessels have yardarms too, you know, and that accursed African wouldn't be the first companion to hang from one for breaking an oath of loyalty. I opened the book to where I had left off and began to write.

The horrible stink from below decks is much diminished, but now I hear things, horrible noises that . . .

I don't know how long I scribbled in that log, until at last I lay my head down and fell asleep in the middle of a passage. I awoke to the sound of gentle creaking. Something was not quite right. I stood and nearly fell as the deck moved suddenly away from me. By God! We were underway. I ran to the door of my cabin and pounded on it.

"Let me out, damn you! Let me out!" There was no response, save another of those chilling groans. I backed away. I remembered Moses' words, and suddenly felt content to stay in my cabin. For the first time, despite being surrounded by privations I wished that I had succumbed to the thirst, hunger and disease that had laid low nearly all my poor crew.

Now there were more noises from outside, a harsh sound of tearing wood, and then my door opened, and in stepped Moses, grinning like a damn fool.

"Greetings, Captain. Or shall I just call you 'Navigator?' It doesn't really matter what we call ourselves, for two things are clear to any mother's son. First, I'm now in command of this ship. Second, I need your help to sail her, for I can't master a ship, for all my years at sea."

"Fine then." I regarded him. "How long have we been underway? What direction are we headed?"

He smiled. "I figure generally west, since we were sailing east when we were becalmed. But I know that generally west is not quite so good as, say, west with a heading of so many degrees, or whatever that course ought to be."

"I'll set us a course for New Providence, then." What choice did I have? I couldn't go much longer myself without food or water, and he'd obviously schemed to turn the crew against me. I started towards the door. He stuck a heavy hand in my chest.

"I think it best if you stay in your cabin, sir—or now I guess I'll be calling you Will, won't I?"

"How am I to take readings from my cabin? I need to go above if I'm to set any sort of useful course for us." He gave me a look, for he'd obviously failed to think that bit of his stratagem through.

"All right, then. Come with me."

I followed him up the short, steep stair and onto the deck and uttered a cry of shock, for there was John Longshanks, gaunt as he'd been the last I'd seen him, yet somehow up and moving about.

"How is it possible?" I started towards old Longshanks, when Moses caught my arm. "I wouldn't get too close. Old John ain't exactly himself these days."

"What do you mean?"

"Well, sir, in addition to being cabin boy and pirate, I already told you I'm also a priest."

"What church would have the likes of you ?"

"Precisely. A priest of the old gods. That's right. Oh, they may have taken the shape and names of your good Christian saints, but they still accept the time honored sacrifices and rites. That they do."

"What do you mean?"

"Zombies, for want of a better term, friend Will. This ship is now crewed by 20 of the living dead."

"My God." Even one so despicable as I was loathe to turn to such unholy recourse. Cannibalism would have been better—at least the poor bastards could have found repose in death.

"Now don't be getting all holy on me—not with your crimes, friend Will. Think of the advantages of this crew."

"What do you mean?"

"A crew of 20 that can't be killed, seeing as they're already dead. A crew what won't insist on shares of booty. Dogs what won't ever get laid low by scurvyor drunk on rum. No feeding them, no pay, no upkeep. Just killers. Every dead man, jack of them."

I stumbled up the steps to the poop deck. The thought of sailing with a crew of dead men was enough to turn my stomach, I'll grant you, but

I also knew that with 20 fewer mouths to feed that same stomach would be full later tonight. Fuller than it had been in a month.

***

We'd been sailing on the course I'd set for nearly a week now. While I can't say I'd gotten used to the miserable creatures that lurched around me, at least I no longer feared them. Perhaps this was due in some part to getting some of my own strength back from having enough food for the last few days. I estimated we would reach New Providence in not more than a day or two. I would then leave the ship to Moses and his infernal crew and find my passage on another vessel, even if it meant working as a common tar for the rest of my days. Maybe I would forsake the sea altogether, in the wake of all I had seen on this last voyage.

It was late, and I made my way down to my cabin. Moses had allowed me to keep it, despite claiming he was in fact captain. I crawled into my berth and was about to nod off to sleep when I heard the door open. Let me keep my cabin, Moses had, but he'd held onto the key.

"Good evening, friend Will."

"What do you want? I peered into the blackness and could see shadows moving behind him.

"Well, I wanted to set something straight between us."

"What's that?"

Moses stepped into the room, followed by three of his decaying crewmen. "You see, old friend, when I told you this here crew didn't require any rations, I may have misspoken."

"Misspoken? How?"

"Well, maybe misspoken isn't the word. It was more of a lie."

"My God."

"That's right, friend Will. They need fresh meat. Raw. About once a week or so. And, well, we haven't made as much headway as I'd hoped." He stepped aside, and I could see the pale bodies creeping toward me, their unblinking eyes and waxy flesh shining in the candlelight. Their teeth clacked as they worked their jaws, with more of the creatures pouring in behind.

"No, no!" I reached for the dagger I now kept beneath my pillow and thrust it to the hilt into John Longshanks. He kept coming at me.

"Kill him! Kill him! His meat's as good as mine!" I cried in a shrill voice I scarce recognized as being my own.

"They can't kill whoever created them, any fool knows that. Just relax, Will. Let it happen. You'll be one of them soon. Once they've had their fill of your flesh, you'll come back to life."

John Gull's Tale

by Stephanie Craig

As I lay dying, I cursed every last one of them. The water came into the brig, cold and black. I had swum to the top of the iron cage, calling out to the cowards. But amongst all the yelling and the flames, no one heard me and no one came to unlock my cell as the ship sank.

It took over an hour for me to die, the water taunting me as it crept up. I had scrabbled so hard against the iron bounds to free myself I broke tooth and nail trying to gain purchase. I screamed until there was no sound left, only the taste of blood in my mouth.

I prayed to God, then to the Devil, then to anyone who would take me. Exhausted, when the water finally rose over the iron bars, I let go. A thousand daggers exploded through my lungs and then I was cold, so cold. As my eyes dimmed, I saw her. So pale and beautiful, white as the moon, her long auburn hair floating around her shining face. She reached out her hand to me. "Will you serve?"

"Anything, anything," I mouthed.

She drew me close, lowered her head to mine and kissed me. Everything went dark.

***

That first year, we waited. The Company gathered its armies, and we were in charge of recruiting in the Atlantic. The galleons were plentiful in coming across the ocean, making for the new worlds, but still it was often a month or two between ships. We were given the *Devil's Hand*, a large full-rigged ship that ran over 150 feet in length. With a crew of 50, we were able to easily keep her, which left plenty of time for other pursuits. We often sang, played cards, and told each other stories to pass the time while we waited for the next catch.

When we discovered a ship, we were usually able to board her within the hour. The captured men were brought into the holds below, and the gold and silver was packed away into the galley stores. Often they had spirits, sometimes wine, sometimes livestock and other stores, which meant there would be a feast that evening. Not that we needed the food, but sometimes it was nice to have the taste of roast pork and the warm glow of rum, to relive what it was like before.

Every so often we were relieved of our cargo by the Company, who sent their shipping fluyts to take the men and metal home.

We served under Captain Roberts at this time, a hard man but fair who generally kept to himself, and we were glad of it. In all, it was a tedious period but pleasant enough, and I was able to make a few friends among the crew as I tended to my daily business. But in my heart, there burnt a slow hot fire and I tended to it often by thinking of how I would get my revenge on the men who killed me. And when I lay down, in my berth to sleep, I would think of the beautiful maiden who had come to save me.

***

I first received news of my old crew when we boarded the *HMS Hunter*, well into our second year. One of the men recognized me as we broke into their holds. His eyes grew wide and he fumbled at the cross strung around his neck.

"Have mercy—oh my God, Johnny, it wasn't me! You have to believe me. I wanted to go back for you but Morgan said you were already dead. Please Johnny, please!" He fell to his knees and started to sob. Parker hit him on the back of the head with his blunderbuss, and he fell to the floor.

"Keep that one above decks," I instructed him. "I'll want him for questioning." I continued to make my way into the hold.

Once we were done and all the cargo had been neatly stowed away on the *Devil's Hand*, I went back above board to see my old friend.

***

Interrogations are always much easier for the dead. Men are generally willing to share their secrets with us, perhaps because they fear the lengths we are capable of going to get our answer.

I found my captive tied to the main mast, muttering prayers and curses as he watched my mates about their business, tending to the sails and setting a new course.

"Come now, no need for that" I said as I approached and signaled for my men to cut him loose. I helped him up and called for a mug of ale. He accepted it greedily. I led him to the stern deck and let him regain his bearings.

"Now, Andrews, tell me what happened that night."

"Well, it was storming, you remember, and we were blasted up on the rocks. There must've been a reef, and we grounded the ship. Evans had left the pitch out from earlier and one of the lanterns knocked over and set it on fire."

"We were trying to put the fires out but the ship kept getting hit by the waves, and we breached the hull."

"I swear, Johnny, by the time we had the jolly boats down, I tried to go back for you, but Morgan said you were already dead. I swear it to you."

I tried to hide my annoyance as I interrupted him. "I know, Andrews, it was Morgan. What happened next?"

"We were able to get 12 men out in the boats, and we made for the shore. The waves tried to dash us on the rocks, but somehow we made it through. We ended up spending a fortnight on the island, but we were fortunate enough to be rescued by a Navy ship when they saw our fires."

"And Fletcher?"

"He made it back. He's got a commission now out in Tahiti. Morgan's with him too, promoted to bosun."

"Do you recall the ship's name?"

"I heard they're on the *HMS Boone*. That's all I know, I swear it."

"Thank you, Andrews, you've been very helpful." I took the mug from him. "Parker, please take our guest to his quarters and see that he's comfortable."

Parker gave poor Andrews another blow to the head and carried his unconscious body to the hold below.

I leaned back against the stern and stared out into the night. As I finished Andrews' ale, I wondered how I would get myself halfway across the world to the Pacific.

***

I resolved to find a way on to the next cargo ship. If each fluyte returned to the home port, then there must be another that was heading out to the South Pacific.

It was 3 long months before I had my chance. We saw the fluyte's topsails just after daybreak.

The Company's cargo ships generally traveled with a captain and a skeleton crew of around 10 to 15 men.

I couldn't come aboard by force, as I needed the Captain and crew to navigate, so I took three of my most loyal men into my confidence and arranged to have myself hidden in one of the larger lockers used to transport gold and silver.

The fluyte's crew carried me aboard with the other cargo, none-the-wiser.

I waited until the sun had set before opening the locker, to be sure that we were far enough from the *Devil's Hand*, and I wouldn't have to face Captain Roberts. Truth be told, I was more afraid of his reproach than his temper, as I was somewhat ashamed to leave his service in this way. However my hatred burned stronger than my regret, and I knew I would have no other way to find Fletcher and Morgan to exact my revenge.

I remained hidden in the bowels of the ship for the duration of my journey to avoid the notice of my hosts. Here and there, we stopped to load cargo from different ships, but other than that, I had free reign of the bay. The treasure was held in the forward hold, and I reasoned that the men must be kept further astern. Two small portholes let in dusty sunlight.

With nothing else to keep me occupied, I plotted the various ways in which I would avenge myself once I found my quarry. Finally, after several months, I could see a mass of tall white clouds in the distance, indicating we would soon be approaching land.

I weighed the prospects of returning to my locker and trying to make my escape in what might be a crowded port. Ultimately, I decided it might be safer to swim to shore, so I climbed up to one of the portholes and looked outside. It was a steep drop of some 40 odd feet, and I would need to stay submersed to escape detection by any crew who might be watching on the port side. I hesitated. I hadn't swum since I was a boy - would I remember how? Steeling myself, I pushed through the wooden frame and fell down to the roaring waters below.

***

As I hit the water, my lungs filled with icy foam and cold jets of bubbles streamed up past my eyes and ears. When the waters cleared, I found myself on the ocean floor. A school of angelfish hurried away and queer glowing jellyfish slowly pulsed through the turquoise waters. I was some hundred feet below the surface. The sunlight shone down in ribbons and cast dappled shadows across the coral and rocks that dotted the sea floor. I would have to swim to the surface to tell which direction would bring me to shore.

A lone figure came into view. With horror, I realized that it was the same pale maiden who had saved me that night. She floated along the sandy floor, her dark hair flowing around her as she stared at me reproachfully. If we were not underwater, I could have sworn that tears rolled down her marble face.

"You promised to serve."

"I did serve. I will serve again," I pleaded. "Just let me finish this one task." I reached out to her.

She did not take my hand.

"You have broken your bond. I do not want you in Our service if your heart lies elsewhere. I release you."

She made a sharp motion with her hand, and I was propelled up to the surface in a torrent of water. I broke through to the air above and soared for a minute or two before I realized I was flying. I looked to my sides and saw long white wings where arms used to be. I had been turned into a gull.

***

People have long held to the notion that sea birds were the trapped souls of sailors, but I hadn't pictured it quite like this. I was still in full possession of my wits, but I could no longer speak. It was quite easy to find the harbor now and before long, I was able to find a cargo ship setting sail for the South Pacific.

I followed them out to sea, and over the course of the next few weeks the sailors came to view me like some kind of pet. They cheered to me and threw me bits of bread and meat.

As I flew alongside them, I plotted how I might find Fletcher and

Morgan, and how I might achieve my objective in my current state. The slow fire of revenge still burnt in my heart.

Yet when I rested amongst the ship's shrouds at night, it was the maiden's face I saw, tears tracking down each perfect cheek. I told myself that I would return to her, when I am done, and prove myself worthy once again. I would make her see that I would do anything for her, anything.

In His Own Way

by Guy Burtenshaw

Sometimes I sit and watch as the ships pass by. Once, many years ago I was in the crew of a man that passed by the name of Captain Zephaniah Calderbank. He was barely noticeable amongst his contemporaries. His successes far outweighed his failures, but his crew were loyal, and, in my once humble opinion, *too* loyal.

The crown was more worried by the likes of Bartholomew Roberts and John Rackham. Calderbank was no more than an irritation in the same way that a mosquito's occasional buzzing might disturb your sleep. He rarely bit hard and was regularly swiped away with a swatter.

A pirate's life was hard, but fare. There were rules, and the most important rule was to respect the rules. When you live by the cutlass, your fellow pirates should be

as family, and you should be able to rely on your family no matter what the day brings. Disrespect the rules and you paid the price. In my opinion, a pirate lives by his reputation and dies by his lack of it. When William Teach raised his flag, people surrendered without a fight— such was the fear his very name instilled. When Calderbank raised his flag, I would swear on my life, if I still had a breath in my body, that I could hear a snigger or two drifting on the breeze.

I started my life in a small town on the Isle of Wight, which you may or may not know as a small island off the coast of Dorset in England. My father had been shot while running from the excise men after landing a boat in a small chime near Ventnor, and I had been sent to school in London by the charity of the church.

As soon as I was old enough, I returned to my former home where

I took my place in the very same gang my father had once sailed with between the isle and Cherbourg in Normandy. It was on a particularly stormy evening that the boat sprung a leak and quite literally fell apart at the seams. Whether fortune or not, I was plucked from the Channel by a passing ship by the name of the *Glory Twig* heading for Bristol.

It was while in Bristol at the Llandoger Trow Inn that Calderbank told me of his plans to take the ship during the night and sail for the Indies where there would be gold for the taking. With little for me to return to, I joined the crew, and in the early hours, we boarded the ship with a crew of eight and headed west.

It was a small crew, but then, it was a small ship Blessed with calm waters, we worked together . Calderbank must have been planning his voyage for a while because he had a flag ready to be raised—black with a white cutlass running horizontally. I could have come up with better, but I wasn't going to argue about a flag.

Our first victory was the capture of a small boat heading away from Port Royal. There was little by the way of valuables on board, but it did provide us with enough food to keep us hidden for a week. When we approached the next boat, the flag was raised, and we were met with gunfire. Our crew was reduced by two men, but we sailed away with a box of gold sovereigns. Back home it would have been enough to live on for a year or two, but we all wanted more. I know greed is a sin, but surely all the gold in the world in the hands of a few that watch while the rest suffer is more of a sin.

In the first few months we were regularly chased by Royal Navy frigates, and on several occasions by other pirates that did not appreciate the competition, but we acquired a fair amount that we concealed on a small uninhabited island Calderbank named Crow Island after the crows heard as we landed. We trusted one another enough to keep the booty together, and the rule was that any one man's portion of the loot passed to the group on expiry.

The capture of a small ship by the name of the *Charles Boone* was our downfall. The ship had seemed sound enough, but as we approached, we could tell not all was well aboard.

Two dead bodies were lying on the deck, mouths agape as though frozen in the midst of anguished cries, glazed eyes staring up at the sky, and when we went below, there were more. The only living person on that ship was the captain, and he was hanging on by the thinnest of threads when Calderbank found him. He appeared to suffer with fever and ranted as I entered his cabin. An empty bottle that stank of rum lay on its side by his hammock, which could only have fuelled whatever fever ran through his veins.

Including myself and Calderbank, there were five of us on that ship, and the only one seemingly unconcerned by the situation was Calderbank. When confronted by a man sweating buckets and shivering like it's mid winter in Dorset, a hundred worries go through your mind, and my list included typhoid.

He kept shouting about something or someone called Tulaji Angre. None of us had ever heard the name before, but that name was all we got before his bloodshot eyes rolled up and he expired.

I found a log amongst his possessions, and the crew found nothing of any value. If any of the ship's deceased crew had anything of any value on them, no one wanted to get too close to find out. Sea faring types hold many superstitions, many of which I will never fully understand even in my present state, but superstitions can keep a man in good health.

We left the ship to drift to whatever destiny fate had planned for it, and I spent the evening reading the log. The ship had left port in the Isle of Bombay over a year before we encountered it. It had made port in several cities since, but if it had ever picked up a cargo at any of them, there had been no trace on the ship. Quite strange for a ship to travel such a distance with nothing of any value.

It was the log's last legible entry that caused me concern, and justifiably so it turned out. A jewel had been taken from a temple called Shri Anantheshwar. That part was straightforward enough even if the name wasn't, and I could hardly judge having chosen piracy as my new profession, but I would like to think I would never take something, however valuable, from a building dedicated to the one up above. Behaviour like that was asking for trouble in anyone's religion.

The log revealed nothing of a man or ship called the Tulaji Angre, and that concerned me as much as the jewel that I had not seen on the ship. I know I said we trusted one another, but Calderbank had entered the captain's cabin first and discovered him dying in his hammock. If there had been such a jewel on board that ship, I was sure that the captain would have kept it in his cabin, and I was certain if Calderbank had seen such a jewel he would have been attracted to it like a moth to a flame. What I could not do was be straight and ask him whether he had found a jewel on the ship. That would be akin to accusing him of stealing from his own crew, and he would not have taken kindly to such an accusation whether it be true or not.

During the days that followed, we were kept in a small cove by a storm that threatened to sink us even in our shelter, and when the wind died and the waters settled, a heavy sea fog had risen around us. I sat on the deck and stared into the fog as it swirled around us forming shapes in my imagination. I saw faces. I saw shapes. I saw many things. And when the dark shape of a boat slowly formed within the fog, I thought it was nothing but my imagination.

When I saw that the crew were all staring at the shape as it emerged from the fog I knew that, if it had ever been in my imagination, it had found a way into the real world. The boat slowly sided up to the Glory Twig and men appeared, their faces concealed in shadow, but they emitted a smell I can only describe as rancid. Even though I could not see their eyes, I felt their gaze, and I felt as though I was rotting from the inside out, my skin tingling as though worms were slivering from my pores. It felt as though my soul was being pulled from my body.

There was no swinging across on ropes or leaping. They simply stepped from their ship onto ours. I could not tell who was in charge, or whether any of them where, but a voice came to us, and the voice said, "You have what cannot be taken."

I put my hand on the hilt of my dagger, which was tucked into a sheaf on my belt, but it did not give me any confidence. I did not think anything we had amongst us could do anything to protect us. The only thing I knew at that moment was that Tulaji Angre had come for his jewel and no quarter would be given.

I looked around for Calderbank and saw, to my horror, he stood on the poop deck pointing his musket towards the darkened figures. In his free hand, he held up a jewel as large as an apple. Even in the gloom, it shone the most deathly of reds. I thought he would throw that jewel at them, but instead he fired his musket and jumped overboard abandoning his ship and his crew.

Our visitors moved across the deck as one, the crew making no attempt to flee. Their screams as they fell forced their way into my eternal memory. I turned, jumped from the ship, and swam. I was never a good swimmer, but with what I could only think of as hell on my tail, I made it ashore and crawled up that beach as far from the fog shrouded waters as my strength would take me.

I thought Calderbank had drowned, but he knelt on the beach staring at the jewel, which he clutched tightly in both hands, the waters lapping around his legs. I watched as the figures appeared behind him and pulled him back into the sea. As he disappeared beneath the surface, he threw the jewel towards the beach where it landed heavily in the sand.

I watched the sea for the whole of the night, and when morning finally arrived, the fog had gone and with it so had the ghostly ship, leaving nothing but the wreckage of the *Glory Twig* floating on the surface of the cove nothing more than flotsam and a forgotten footnote in history. The jewel remained where it had landed, and I left it there. I dared not touch it even though it kept me prisoner on that island.

The only drinkable water was from the rain that infrequently fell, and the only food was the tough leaves of the plants. There were fish in the sea, but I had no boat, and I was not going to set one foot in that water. Given the choice of the island or hell, I chose the island. On nights when the fog returns, the dark shape of that ship appears and on its deck its crew stares at me, boring into what remains of my soul with their gaze.

I do not know when my soul and body parted company, only that one day I no longer felt the pain of thirst. There was only me and that ship, and I no longer needed the fog to see it. It drifted in the cove seeking the return of the jewel, its crew unable to set foot on land, me unable to enter the water. Locked forever in a game of time, the silence of the night is broken only by the occasional cries of Calderbank and his crew calling out from hell.

I sit and I watch as the ships pass by. I watch as they grow on the horizon and fade into the distance. The days pass into weeks, the weeks into months, the months into years and beyond that time is meaningless. How long I have remained trapped on the island no longer seems to be important. One day someone will arrive and find that stone buried in the sand, and they will take it for themselves, and when they do, my tormentors will leave me be. I hope when that day comes my soul will be allowed to pass in the right direction. The island is a lonely place, but there are far worse places. The cries from beyond tell me so.

Shores of Leguan Island

by Stewart Hotson

I didn't realise the curse was real until just a few days before I died. I was a seaman, a buccaneer with a proper charter from his Majesty. The captain kept the seal in a chest in his cabin and showed it when the quartermaster brought new crew on board. He wasn't a bad man was Captain Wainwright even if he did take four shares to our one. He worked to that sense of British Honour that makes us better than those deceitful papists we vie with along the coasts of the Americas. Not for us the murder of merchants and taking hostage of women and children, and he would never allow us to set them adrift without hope of reaching port.

Wainwright was fearsome in a fight, even if he was a toff, and many a brigand of the rougher sort regretted tangling with us in the hopes of a golden reward from the Spanish Queen or the French Emperor. If the captain was a devil in an engagement, Smith the quartermaster was as implacable with us, his mates. Some dog by the name of Fletcher ripped the dress from some pretty young Spanish girl, and Smith had the man scourged and dumped at a plantation for his insubordination. The girl's father was given the five shillings we got for Fletcher's sorry hide to cover the dishonour. We might not have liked it but they was men we could respect, men who we knew would fight for us who would share good fortune with us. I, for one, threw my lot in with them every time the question was put on who should be in charge.

What I'm trying to say is that we were a crew in good order, fighting for the crown and never did we kill anyone who didn't come at us with murder in their guts. So now I find myself wandering the shores of Leguan Island, palm fronds waving in the sordid breeze, trying to figure out what and where we went wrong. It didn't take me long to plumb the reason and I'll tell you this for free; all of us is doomed now, condemned for the evil we did one old woman.

I wasn't no Christian child growing up, even if I did receive my share of canings at the hands of nuns. They never beat more than the fear of being caught into my bones. It was Captain Wainwright who made me see that my ways could serve the King and by that, find some measure of salvation in the brutish life I found myself suited to. I guess, pleasing God himself, that I was always outside that assembly of the saints, but even if that weren't the case what happened, what brought us all low, would have thrust us beyond the reach of the captain of our souls. Hell, we didn't even reckon on what we'd done till it was too late to do anything but face our end, in whatever manner we decided for ourselves. For me, it was trying to do right by the old Higue but that was as futile as looking a black who thinks being a slave is a good idea.

Now, afore you judge me by the light of what I'm going to tell you, I want you to know this: my part in this story is one of foolishness but not malice or evil. If my mate was the one who sinned while I stood by, then that's my shame, but his fault. This I swear on Nelson's Honour: if I had an inkling of what Stoop would do, I would have gone straight to Smith and had him stopped, blood brother or not.

It started when we visited this cursed island the time before we died. The northern coast of that mosquito infested, jungled land was full of inlets and coves where a sloop of war like the *Reckoning* could tie up and wait for her prey. At the southern end of the Caribbean, it's also the perfect spot to lie low when some naval captain, full of the joys of his command, looked to put us into Davy Jones' locker. She was, and still is, a beauty and I hope it's someone worthwhile who finds her lolling half a mile from where I'm fated to wander. 75 feet long, shallow draft and a displacement of just 80 tons. With her ten guns we could take just about whatever we were interested in—bullion, gold or silver and promissory notes, land charges and spices. We were in the habit of throwing the rest over the side. There's no sense in leaving what we don't want for the papists to salve their wounded pride.

In describing the ship to you, as she's moored just off the coast, empty of human life, I'm reminded of how just how different the jungle appears to me now. I can see spirits flitting between the trees, shapes and colours coalescing and warping, merging and conquering one another all around;

a veritable city of sprites no rational man would give credence to. They take no notice of us, nor do we try to talk with them. Monkeys share branches with homunculi, while pineapples grow alongside pulsating garish fruits of this nether world that give their earthly companions the sudden homely attractiveness of the humble British pear. I think that yesterday a Moongazer came towering through our motley camp, face turned skywards, oblivious to our invasion of his world. None of us was fool enough to disturb his meditations.

It was not far from here that we moored that night the curse was brought down upon our heads. We'd fled south after a successful raid on a Spanish caravel carrying cloth and some small amount of silver between fortified positions among the islands. A well crewed brig chased us for a week, but we were too fast. Wainwright knew his business too well for them to have a hope of catching us once we'd put our minds to it. You might think it was a straight race but that'd only give them our final destination and remove the point of being nimble in the first place. Instead we tacked west and then east, always ahead of them until we vanished over their horizon, leaving them casting about at random hoping to the pope we'd eventually make our way north again so they could intercept us. That there's the genius of the south Americas, if you find a safe berth then you don't need to run back to British waters for safety.

Some of us missed the comforts of a proper port; the women, the grog and the freedom to spend our spoils. Smith always reckoned that we were kings of our own towns when we did put in because the times between were longer and the spoils added up to greater than for the crews of those sloops that hid out in the crowds after every attempt at taking the enemy. We couldn't say he was wrong even if our loins wished it were otherwise.

Nothing untoward happened when we disembarked onto the island, the Captain made the distribution in the rolls so we all knew what we were due, and Smith rationed out enough rum so that we could enjoy ourselves. Elliot, who passed for the ship's barber, knew enough of the local fruits to find sweet stuff to add to our rations of meal and dried meat. Traps were set for the following morning; the giant rats here make the mouth water even if I'd never tell anyone proper what we were eating. All in all, we had a good time and were no more concerned by the jungle around us than any other time we pulled in. It was when Stoop was asked by Smith to go find more wood fit for burning that we started taking on water. Stoop was a young man and the *Reckoning* was his first ship. He'd been born, abandoned and grown up in the streets of Nassau before trying to pick Smith's pocket one night we were ashore there. Smith is not the sort to take young boys fleecing him. He gave Stoop such a beating his back's never been straight since. I don't know why but he then offered Stoop a spot on the rolls, and Stoop took him at his word.

Smith was already calling him Stoop when he was carried aboard by a couple of seamen and he's never gone by any other name. He could be an evil little fuck, especially ashore when he thought no one was looking at what he was up to. However, we were thick as thieves at sea, always partnering for a boarding as he was as vicious as a hungry ferret in a bag of mice when the situation demanded.

Now Stoop took me and Charlie with him into the trees that crowded the centre of the island like lost children in a market. Vines, creepers, thorns and flowers choked them but even though it was dark, we unsheathed our machetes and hacked our way through the growth looking for a fallen tree. Truly rotten wood would be too damp to take fire. We looked for dead wood that the rains thereabouts hadn't already softened into so many fragments still held together by nothing more than the memory of being a tree.

All of a sudden Charlie shouted out like a in a high pitched voice. Me and Stoop found him quivering like he seen his own mum floating through the undergrowth.

"You see it?" he asked us, his voice quavering.

"See what you Spanish whore?" said Stoop, the sneer on his face plain even in the dank light of the moonlight jungle.

Charlie said nothing, his eyes fixed on some spot in the woods past us and slowly, horrible like, he raised his hand and pointed.

We turned then, and I am not ashamed to say I lost control of my bowels without even knowing it till later. There, hovering a few feet from Charlie's outstretched finger was a ball of fire bobbing about gently at head height. We all heard tales of willow the wisp at sea— those balls of light that come to scare crooked men honest during those merciless storms that strike from the darkest storm cells out at sea, but this was nothing like that. I, myself, had seen one once as it floated across the roaring waves swept down to the deck before swirling up and around the mizzen mast. Half way up it simply disappeared like it had never been.

The thing in front of us was all yellow, about the size of a coconut with little licks of flame flapping from its surface. It hung there, and I felt my spine crawl. It had no eyes but all three of us knew it was watching. I felt like a school teacher was taking my measure, and it made me sick to my bones. I was less nervous than Charlie, and unlike him, I was moved to approach it, but Stoop was having none of that. "Be gone, Devil!" he shouted at it. "We want none of your sort here. This is our island." He ran at it, waving his machete and to my utter amazement, the globe fell back under his advance. He whooped in that joy I've seen in his eyes when blood was going to be spilt. Before I knew it, I was following him through the trees as he chased the flame toward the centre of the island.

We couldn't have run more than three hundred yards, but in among those trees it might as well have been three miles. All of a sudden, I came upon Stoop stood, slack jawed, in the twilight of the evening looking up into the branches of a dead tree. I squinted, trying to make out what he'd seen, and as I did he started laughing like a jackal, swinging his machete and dancing as if he just discovered Eldorado. Meanwhile I couldn't believe my eyes 'cause there in the fork of the trunk hung what appeared to be a ragged sack, swaying in the evening breeze coming off the sea. As I stared, stepping closer, I realised it wasn't any old sack but the slack skin of some poor wretch left there all alone.

"Poor sod," said I, but this caused Stoop to cackle all the louder. He strode past me and started climbing the tree. I looked around but couldn't see any sign of the fire we'd been following. Stoop shouted at me to catch, so I put myself under him. With a groan I took the weight of the sagging body as he unhitched it from the tree. The weight of it forced me to my knees. The thing had been boned and all that was left was the skin and scraps of flesh. I wasn't sure, but reckoned it belonged to some old woman, there were certainly flabby breasts and wrinkles aplenty. Coarse hair moved under my fingers, it was all I could do not to drop the coat of skin right there. Stoop leapt from the tree and took the body.

"It's an old higue," he said with glee. I had no idea what he was talking about, but I do remember that his voice rasped with triumph and delight. I watched as he held out the body like one might a coat you were going to buy on shore leave. He pulled it this way and that; it was just like a jacket made from someone's body.

"What are you going to do?" I asked.

"Burn it," he said firmly. I must have nodded because next thing I remember is us walking back toward the camp, stopping to find Charlie on the way. The poor wretch didn't speak again for the rest of his days, not that ever came near us after that.

Finding the camp making merry we were challenged for not bringing no wood back with us, but those with most to shout about shut their traps when they saw what Stoop carried. A silence spread out from him like a ripple in a puddle. The wallowing quiet, naturally, brought Wainwright and Smith to see what the fuss was that had laid everyone low.

"What've you got?" asked Smith, his voice neutral and clear. Wainwright stood just behind him, arms folded across his chest, eyes glittering in the firelight as he pondered what we'd brought into camp.

"It's an old higue," said Stoop, his voice less certain but more defiant because of it.

Smith nodded but Wainwright, proper Englishman that he was, said, "And what, pray tell, is that?"

Stoop looked at Smith who inclined his head ever so slightly I reckon most missed it but then he turned and said to Wainwright "Stoop's business Captain, after he's collected his wood, he's going to burn that. Nothing for us to concern ourselves with."

Wainwright might have been the best fighter I ever seen, but it don't mean he was all muscles and no fat, nor that he was the cleverest man on deck. He watched Stoop's face and licked his lips. We all knew his indecision at moments like this. Give him a situation he knew, and he'd beat any man put against him. Yet new stuff, things he didn't know, and he was as like to freeze, unable to choose left or right. You could see the Christian soul in him objecting to what they wanted to do, that it wasn't right to burn a body, but he knew the rules like the rest of us. Out of combat, the quartermaster was the boss of us all. The moments stretched out and just when I thought to myself that he would stand there forever, he clicked his heels together softly and, whipping around, returned to the fire where he'd left his grog unattended.

The rest of the crew knew the matter was settled, but unlike Wainwright, most of them wanted to see the spectacle for themselves. I reckon a third of us knew then what an higue was, and they that did crowded round closest to Stoop, sighs of fearful awe on their lips.

Yet before Stoop could make good on their anticipation, Smith's voice rose over the men's hubbub. "Stoop, you owe me wood. That's your duty. Only when that is served will you be granted leave to attend to personal matters."

Stoop crouched down and put the sad sack of skin onto the ground with exaggerated care, "Aye sir." He never left camp though because as Smith was telling the others to stay away from Stoop's burden the ball of fire floated into view. It crackled as it came, and it came quick this time, determined it was. The men fell back with cries of alarm, leaving just me, Smith, and Stoop, who stood near the body. The flame slid past us to stop in the air over the woman's shell. Then it was gone. Gasps added to the evening chorus. I remember seeing Wainwright watching from his fire, tankard in one hand, face still as he took it all in.

Then nothing. No explosion, no horrors, just cicadas and monkeys crying in the gloom.

"Sweet Jesus," said someone as the sack of flesh started twitching like it was filled with snakes or worms. The extremities flicked out like whips and the whole sheath of skin flailed to the sound of grinding bones. The crew of the *Reckoning* have seen their share of guts, but I wasn't the only one to heave my stomach onto the dirt at the sight.

Those who knew what she was started shouting "Rice! Where's some rice?" I thought them the most cracked of all at the time, but if only we could have listened to them, we might have stopped our doom in its tracks before it had begun.

The body stretched out now, the head full again of skull and jawbone. Her legs straightened, and her arms pushed at the ground. My eyes watered to see the woman stand to her feet, an inevitability to it that chilled my soul. Her eyes were black as Stoop's back teeth. They seemed to drink insatiably at the evening, daring us to return her gaze. Beside me Stoop heaved his machete in his hands but didn't move. She opened her mouth, singing in some heathen tongue I didn't understand. I could feel the ground around me soften, wrinkling as if alive, but I couldn't move. Her song kept me where I was, looking at her face as she grinned her godless harmonies over our souls.

Stoop advanced and slashed wildly at her. She cowered back under his cuts, but there was no blood, no splashing of gore and moments later she stood upright again, screamed her song to the night as she backhanded him across the face. Stoop went flying backwards. It was like she had thrown a baby across a room, and he landed with a tumbling rush at my feet.

"Spawn!" came a cry from behind me and swift as death himself,

Wainwright flew past me, sabre in hand to run her through. His eyes were full of fire. She stumbled backwards but didn't stop singing.

"No!" shouted Stoop in dismay and crawled forwards. My hand went to his arm, he looked at me, terror streaming from his eyes. "Burn her," he whispered.

I looked back to see Smith, Wainwright and our weapons master Tomlinson engaging her in a terrible one-sided melee. They thrust their weapons into her again and again, but although each blow now drew forth dribbling black liquid, she showed no signs of being done in. They were more disciplined than Stoop and surrounded her, avoiding her wild swings easily, but none of them could end her. Of those who hadn't fled to the ends of the island, none came close.

I grabbed a branch from the dying fires and ran to the fight. I hovered at the edge until the moment presented itself and, seeing my chance, hit her a solid blow with the flaming end. We were all thrown back by the higue who exploded like a Catherine wheel on November 5th. She lashed out, but her three assailants had fallen back, and all of us stood, gawping at her as she burned with the fizz and crackle of fat boiling in the heat.

Instead of dying she gathered herself and ran in a mad ungainly dash for the jungle. As you can imagine, none of us followed after her.

People collapsed to their haunches in the wake of her departure. Sighs, weeping, and silence followed in her train. Eventually the fires started to sputter out which served to jerked us out of our timid reverie; none of us was prepared to be alone in the dark that night. Men gathered themselves and, in groups of at least four or five, they went out to find more wood with an alacrity Smith must have wished they'd express on deck.

Sleep was fitful in the days after, even though we heaved off Leguan with the first tide. Like some pact had been signed between us, none of us talked of what had happened. At first, it appeared we had escaped with our lives and souls intact. Not a few of us found a church when we reached British soil, hats clutched at our breasts and thankful for our lives.

Yet not everything was right with the *Reckoning*. We couldn't make a haul; the wind would abandon us when we sighted prey. The weather would close on us when it was our turn to flee and each of us had accidents as if we were ham fisted idiots. It was weeks later, when we ventured into a port, limping from an unlucky cannonade hit, that our suspicions were confirmed. I was walking with Stoop through the market when an elderly man of the local tribes started shouting at us. This was no concern of ours so we ignored the Indian. He was similarly unperturbed by our indifference, following us around until we confronted him. Neither me nor Stoop spoke his lingo, but a stranger in the market approached and offered to tell us what he said.

We weren't for paying the fellow, but he insisted that we needed to know what he had to say. Satisfied we weren't being done over we listened.

"You men trespassed the home of a higue," started the interpreter as a crowd began gathering around us. Murmurs accompanied each sentence the old man said. "You did not throw rice , nor did you escape." At another time, I would have snorted my disdain, but we all knew what we'd seen and none of us had spoken of it. Whatever sorcery this man had at his wit, we knew he was right.

"You are cursed twice over," said the elder, trembling as he spoke, the people around us drew back at his utterance, and I wanted nothing more than to be on the *Reckoning* and away. "Once for trespass and twice for attacking her but not driving her away as should be done." He looked around the market, his eyes like beetles burrowed into his face as he squinted in the sunlight. "I name you *Jumbee*. I drive you from here. Be gone from us and take your curses with you."

The people scattered away from us, shouting at the name *Jumbee*. Even I knew it was what the locals called the worst of evil spirits. Stoop and I looked at one another as dread settled in our stomachs and knew we had just minutes before the crowd returned with weapons to slaughter us where we stood. We weren't fools and took to our heels as fast as we could back to port.

Smith listened to our story then gave the command to make the ship ready to sail immediately. It wasn't a moment too soon either. We watched as hundreds of dark skinned Indians gathered on the quays in silence, blades glinting in the sun, as we skimmed out of the harbour into the sapphire waters of the Caribbean.

Wainwright was determined to take us back to Leguan and none of us dared disagree with his sentiment. We knew we were done for if we couldn't make it right with this demon. For once, the wind was with us but McKillick fell sick with fever, vomiting and dysentery two days from Leguan. His sickness spread before Eliot confined him to his bunk below decks. He died before the next morning. His groaning pleas for mercy, as he rolled in his bed, made us all fear for our souls. By lunchtime, three more men had succumbed, and the disease spread like a fire through flax. Even as we moored in the place we once considered a haven, barely a dozen of us were still hale.

Wainwright said nothing but Stoop took the lead with us following him through the jungle to where Charlie had first spied the higue, glowing as a ball of fire. We found the tree where the higue's body had hung and loitered there, hoping some idea of what should be done would present itself to us. Smith complained of feeling ill and truth be told, I too was starting to feel chilled in that unforgiving tropical heat. Given how quickly the others expired after first succumbing to fever, I reckoned had a scant few hours left on this earth.

Wainwright fished a bible from his jerkin and knelt before the tree. Heavy rain started to fall and the pages tore as he tried to turn them. He read a psalm; the one that talked about the valley of death, but after a while, he fell silent and hung his head. I clasped my hands to my arms and joined the Captain on the ground. I closed my eyes, but I wasn't a godly man and didn't know how to pray, so I kept my trap shut and hoped Wainwright was right enough with God for us both.

Faintly cutting through the sounds of the jungle came the clip of a horse. At first I thought it must be something else, but it got louder and nearer. Opening my eyes, I saw we were all looking out for the arrival of the horse and its rider. The smell of rotting flesh wafted toward us and bursting from the trees came a pale, gut coloured horse, eyes vivid purple, mouth dripping with violet froth. Around me men sighed; our damnation stood before us. It paced the ground in a circle around us and one by one the men quietly collapsed, their already cold bodies still as if they'd been dead for hours. I didn't last any longer and with a feeling of my bladder emptying the world fell away. My last sight was of Wainwright stood over me crossing himself. It didn't save him. I guess none of us were what you'd called righteous, no matter what the King said.

So now I wander this island, constrained from stepping out onto the water and escaping. I don't know how long we're going to be here but the *Jumbee* left us some time ago and hasn't returned. For the time being I'm trying to learn about the spirits that live here like it was their Eden. When I was alive I might not have been proper but I was a privateer— given license by the king. Now I'm not even a privateer, there's no charter that can save types like us.

Spectre of the Eridanus

by Kate Monroe

20th August, 1857

Thus begins the personal journal of Julian Ashton, Esquire; in which I shall attempt to convey the full horror of the days I spent on board the Eridanus *and the unfortunate fate which befell me.*

I

This tale—which I assure you, dear reader, is entirely true and painfully honest!—began on a wild and stormy night deep in the bosom of the Atlantic Ocean. As a passenger on board the *HMS Tantalus*, I had endured many such nights on the course of our voyage; but even as a novice sailor, I recognised this was something else entirely.

Vicious winds whipped around our vessel, buffeting it from side to side amongst the churning waves of the ocean beneath us. Thunder rolled in the raging skies above, and the similar countenance of the whiskered captain when he escorted me to my cabin below deck told me all I needed to know. It was only a matter of time before the storm's assault would become too much for the *HMS Tantalus* to bear.

The events of the hours that followed are somewhat hazy in my mind, I am afraid. I recall there was no sense in abandoning ship, for the waves that tossed the ship about like no more than a child's plaything in a bathtub were so violent that a smaller craft would stand no chance of withstanding them. I confess I was terribly afraid and convinced I would meet my end that very night.

Jumbled images flash through my mind now as I force myself to recall them. I remember the haunting cry of the crew's screams overhead as they fought to steer the ship through the storm. I saw one young lad, no more than fourteen, tumble past my cabin window to be devoured by the waves that swallowed him. The salty ocean slammed up against the ship over and over again, and though she and her crew battled valiantly, as I recited the Lord's Prayer for the seventh time she could hold out no longer.

With a shuddering creak, the hull was rent into a dozen pieces.

Though my terror threatened to overcome all my good sense, I retained the wits to cling to an empty crate for a makeshift float as the wood that was the only defence between me and the storm was ripped away. As the numerous parts of the *HMS Tantalus* plummeted to their grave, a vicious riptide swirled through my cabin and dragged me out into the ocean's bitter grip.

I could barely even breathe, let alone retain any clarity of thought. Helpless, I simply held onto the crate and allowed the storm to buffet me at its will. Within moments all sight of the ship and its crew was lost to me as I was pulled away from the wreckage. All I could do was pray, and to my amazement it seemed a guardian angel swam alongside me that night.

When the storm finally ceased its relentless assault of my exhausted body, the clouds parted overhead to allow the weak moonlight to shine down upon the horizon—and there, to my great joy, was a glimpse of land. The calming current was carrying me towards the small island and I gladly submitted to it, allowing it to deliver me to the sandy shore where I found the strength to drag myself away from the water before my eyes closed and I gave myself over to the merciful black mist that called to me. I knew nothing more until a deep voice summoned me back to consciousness.

"To your feet, my good man. The world is not yet through with you."

I stared up in disbelief at the man towering over me, framed by the new sun at his back. His strong jaw was set in determination, and his whiskers twitched as I gaped wordlessly. At an estimate, I would place him in his early forties. His tanned skin was beginning to display the first signs of time's ravage, and the black hair that hung in loose waves around his shoulders was streaked with whispers of white. None of that, though, lessened the impact or authority of his piercing stare. His grey eyes gleamed with something I could not put name to, though if pressed I would have been inclined to call it amusement as he held out his hand to me.

"I am Judson Fox, captain of the *Eridanus.*"

I stammered out my name and my fervent thanks as he pulled me up and gestured to the airship currently resting in the glistening waters behind us. The contrast to the night before could not have been more marked. All trace of the ocean's raging fury had been wiped away to leave a calm serenity that recalled to me precisely what had fostered my love for the seas in the first place.

"Will you accept my offer of a cabin on board the *Eridanus,* good sir?"

I eagerly accepted, thinking myself fortunate beyond words that Captain Fox had found me. What a fool I was.

II

The *Eridanus* was a thing of great beauty. My previous transport faded in comparison to her vast magnificence; everything from the precisely carved hull to the air balloon tethered to her decks spoke of extravagance and wonder. My eyes were wide as I tried to greedily drink it all in, forgetting even my need for rest and sustenance to recover from the damage the storm had wreaked upon me in the face of the glory of the ship.

Captain Fox nodded in evident approval when I spoke my admiration for his vessel, but our talk soon turned to the future. Hesitantly, I enquired if he was due to sail near England any time soon.

"I had not planned to," said he, "but I am more than willing to provide you with passage home, sir. In return all I ask is that you assist with the tasks necessary for the smooth running of a vessel like the *Eridanus.*"

I gladly accepted his offer as he steered me below deck, telling me that before he took me to my cabin he wanted to show me where he slept in case I had need of him at all. The room he directed me into was airy and handsome, but my gaze was drawn to where a fair-haired woman was seated at the desk beneath the round window, staring out to sea.

She did not even glance up when we entered the room; indeed, the only sign she gave that she was aware of our presence in any way was a barely perceptible shudder when the captain laid a cold hand on her shoulder. "My lady," he announced, placing what seemed to be a deliberate stress on the possessive term. "Arabella, my dear, rise to your feet and greet my new guest."

"Guest, captain?" Her faint voice was melodious and steady, despite its delicacy. Still she did not look around at us, even as she spoke. "Or do you perhaps mean another prisoner like me on this godforsaken ship?"

My eyes widened as storm clouds descended to darken his countenance. "A prisoner?" he echoed, his dark brows knitted together menacingly. "But you are not a prisoner here. My dear, you are confused again."

She sighed heavily and folded her hands together in her lap, neither confirming nor denying his grim assertion. As she shifted in her high-backed seat, a soft clink of metal on wood from beneath her elaborate skirts drew my gaze downwards, but the captain moved across to block my view. He lowered his head towards hers and I saw her breath quicken with what could only be fear. "Arabella?" he said quietly, the menace in the word in no way lessened by the tenderness with which he spoke it. "I am taking Mr. Ashton to his quarters now to recover from his ordeal. When I return, you are to be ready to take dinner with me."

She did not speak that I could hear, but he seemed satisfied with the mere lack of dissent. "One more thing before I go, my dear," said he. "I think you should apologise to our *guest* for alarming him so with your foolish words." He mouthed something else that was clearly not for me to hear and a solitary tear rolled down her pale face as he helped her to her feet and turned her to face me.

Arabella swallowed hard, but she lifted her eyes to look up at me through lowered lashes. Dumbstruck by the beauty of her face and the misery in the breathtaking depths of her blue eyes, I could not help but take a step backward—and I do not think the captain failed to note my reaction. His face darkened yet further and his hand tightened around her arm as she spoke.

"I am sorry for any distress I caused you, Mr. Ashton," she whispered, a waver to her voice that wrenched at my heart. I took a step towards her in order to assure her I held no grudge, but the captain forced her back into the seat and steered me out of the cabin before I could tell her so.

As he guided me through the ship's narrow corridors, he bowed his head towards mine confidingly. "You will have to forgive my lady. She is easily confused, to my everlasting grief. For her own safety I keep her secluded in the cabin; as you saw, when meeting people she is not familiar with it overwhelms her."

I could not help but feel uneasy with his explanation. "Is Arabella your wife, captain?" I asked.

"In the eyes of the law? No." The captain ran his thumb along the strong line of his jaw and smiled; a smile that was entirely lacking in humour. "But in every other way she is mine, Ashton. Do you understand?"

I nodded, and his smile widened as we came to a halt in front of a heavy oaken door.

"Excellent. Your cabin, good sir. I trust that you will find it comfortable."

Before I could even thank him he had ushered me inside and closed the door behind me - and I heard the distinctive sound of a key clicking in the lock.

It seemed the lady was right. For a reason I could not fathom, I was Captain Fox's prisoner.

III

Despite my unease, I slept through the day. When I awoke the moon was high in the cloudless sky and its pale rays cast enough illumination over my small cabin that I could not return to sleep.

I rose from my bed and tried the door, but it was immovable. As I feared, the captain had indeed locked me in. Before I could even begin to dwell upon the consequences of his actions, though, a piercing scream smashed through the still of the night.

My heart lost a beat as I staggered backwards before regaining my composure and hammering at my door. No-one came, even as another scream rang out to echo inside my head. I knew I would never forget the sound of it, for every last note of it was drenched in a terror I could never even comprehend until that moment, regardless of all I had been through.

The longest hour of my life passed before my frantic calls were finally answered. The screams had long since died away, but they were etched forever into my memory. As the captain unlocked and opened my door, I seized hold of his shirt in reckless abandon and pleaded with him to tell me what it was I had heard.

But he only smiled and shook his head. "Men often say that the seas are haunted, Ashton. Mayhap you merely heard the ghost of the *Eridanus.*"

"I do not think it was a ghost, sir!"

His grey eyes narrowed as he fixed them intently upon me. "Then what, pray tell, do you suppose it was?"

My mind could summon up only one conclusion, but I dared not put direct voice to my suspicion; for if I was right, it could have only one cause. I bowed my head to evade his piercing stare as I spoke quietly to the floor. "How is your lady tonight, captain? I hope she was not troubled by the sounds that so disturbed me."

"Arabella sleeps soundly in my bed, Ashton. I know that to be a certainty, for I came to you directly from her."

When I dared look up again, there was a gleam in his eyes that sent a shiver down the length of my spine

~

(Publisher's note) Regretfully, the next two pages are indecipherable, having been spoiled by the seawater that had leaked into the bottle the journal was found in.

The narrative resumes here.

~

...though I applied myself to the tasks that the captain set me over the next few days and outwardly accepted his explanations, it was with a heavy heart and a dulled spirit. Misery pervaded every last inch of the hull of the *Eridanus*, and its black cloud hung over me with an unerring constancy that sapped at my strength.

Above all else, the mystery of the screams I was sure came from the captain's lady each night occupied my fretful mind.

IV

On my fourth night aboard the *Eridanus* I furtively slipped below deck while the captain was barking his orders to the crew, for I had heard a low and mournful cry. Its tones were so similar to that which haunted my nights that I could not repress an answering cry of my own as I hastened towards it source.

It was as I had suspected. It came from Captain Fox's own cabin— and being that he was at the helm, I knew precisely from whom it came.

"My lady?" With a thrill of anticipation I pushed open the door and dashed to Arabella's side, for she was doubled over where she stood and her face was contorted in agony. "My lady, what ails you? If you are in pain, perhaps I should summon the captain -"

"No!"

Her terrified cry spoke volumes, despite its solitary syllable. Impulsively I caught her hands in mine. I clasped them against my chest as I threw caution to the wind and spoke the words I was convinced of. "You are not happy here, my lady; indeed, I have not even seen you smile since I arrived!"

"As a caged bird does not sing, thus I do not smile."

Her cryptic words determined my mind. "Tell me, Arabella," said I. "Tell me your story."

She retook her customary seat at the desk behind her. A glass of wine sat there, half-empty, and she picked it up to swirl the blood-red liquid around as she began to speak. "It began ten months ago. I was sailing with my brother back to England when Captain Fox led an attack upon our vessel. He and his pirate crew plundered the cargo and murdered all the men on board, my brother included; and then the captain claimed me for his own bounty."

"Claimed you?"

Her clouded eyes flickered to the bed behind us and I understood. I opened my mouth, but no words would come to express my outrage. Arabella tilted her head to the side and nodded in comprehension of all I felt; for, after all, it must be a hundred times more horrific for she who lived all I was imagining. She lifted the wine glass to her lips and her sleeve fell back to expose a circlet of chafed skin around both her slender wrists.

Though a moment before I would not have thought it possible, my heart pounded even more wildly as I crouched down next to her. "My lady, what is this?"

"The captain does not trust me not to flee while he sleeps." Her lips barely moved as she spoke, but the horror in her eyes spoke more eloquently than any fervent declaration possibly could.

My breath caught in my constricted throat. Unable to stop myself, I reached out and took hold of her hand to lift it up towards the light of the gas lamp. A knot of tense fury tightened around my heart, causing it to thud wildly out of time, for the marks that marred her impossibly soft skin seemed to have only one possible cause.

"Does he bind you, Arabella?"

A soft and sorrowful sigh drifted from her wine-stained lips as I let her hand fall back to her side. "Every night, sir. He restrains my wrists and takes his pleasure from me before tying me to the bedpost while he rests. He is right to do so, for if I had my autonomy I would plunge a knife through his black heart, futile though that would be, then throw myself overboard to escape the memories of the hell he has put me through."

I believed her implicitly. "And what of your days, my lady?"

"The days I spend chained to the desk in his cabin; there is enough length that I might walk around and attend to my physical needs, but I am trapped here as surely as the poor animals that pace the confines of London's zoological gardens—as are you."

"I am not chained, Arabella!"

Her shoulders rose and fell. "But you are just as incapable of leaving as I am, sir. The captain locks your door while you sleep because he does not intend to release you, not to keep you safe. He wants to make use of you to crew his ship; why would he willingly release an able-bodied, living man? None of those who crew the *Eridanus* are here by choice."

There was so much more I wanted and needed to say to her in the face of her revelations, but the sound of footsteps overhead heralded the captain's return. Arabella blanched and leapt up to usher me to the door, her chains clinking around her bare feet as she did so. "Sir, you should not be here! If Judson discovers you alone with me..."

She trailed off and my stomach lurched painfully. "Arabella -"

A tear rolled down her pale face. "Julian, please! For my sake if not your own, you must leave!"

Her desperate entreaty tugged at something deep inside me. Though I wanted to stay and defend her, I saw the sense in her words. I left her to the captain's tender care.

Later that night her sobbed pleas were louder than ever, carrying through the ship as I laid tossing and turning in my bed as if it was me alone she called out to.

I did not sleep.

V

When dawn eventually arrived, it brought with it the utter conviction I had to free Arabella from her miserable fate bound to the captain she so clearly feared and detested. To my amazement, when I went above deck in search of him it was to find him at the helm with the lady herself at his side.

He greeted me with a smile even as his arm tightened possessively around her waist. "We near the coast of Greenland, Ashton. I thought that my lady would care for an excursion today, so we will be docking at the shore."

My surprise at his words must have been apparent, for I was sure spending the day with him as well as the night was the very last thing she desired. "An excursion?" I repeated slowly.

"Can you not see how pale she is? Clearly she is pining for the sunshine."

I could not restrain myself. "The *sunshine*? Sir, the lady is pining for her freedom—is it not plain to see how miserable she is? I am convinced that is the cause of her fatigue and ill pallor."

His face darkened as he turned to her. "Tell our guest it is not so, Arabella!"

"You know I am miserable, captain." Her words were so low and softly spoken that we both had to strain to hear them. "Do I not tell you so every evening and plead with you to release me from this ship?"

Upon seeing the acerbic rage contorting the captain's brow, I deeply regretted my impulsive rebuke. He did not answer her. Instead, he strode towards a storage locker near the mast and pulled out a contraption, the likes of which I had never seen before. His grey eyes burned ferociously as he turned a key to wind its clockwork engine before turning back to the trembling lady at the helm.

"Arabella, you will come with me to scout out the sea ahead."

He fastened the leather straps around his chest, and stunned comprehension dawned upon me as two vast feathered wings spread out behind him. The captain intended to fly with his lady. Against my will I felt a grudging admiration for the man, despite his myriad flaws, for the device was remarkable. I had seen nothing like it before, and were it not for the circumstances I would have been glad to see its operation and inspect it further. My eyes, though, were fixed firmly upon Arabella, for still she had not moved.

"Come, Arabella!" he said impatiently.

She lifted her head to look him in the eye. "No, Judson. I will not go with you."

The captain tossed the contraption to the deck and strode back towards her with a chilling fury etched into his face as he backed her up against one of the steel ropes tethering the air balloon to the ship. She cried out, but he only laughed. Then as she beat her fists wildly against his chest and he seized a handful of her hair to drag her back below deck, the *Eridanus* rocked wildly to the port side.

The terrified scream of a deckhand who was thrown overboard with the movement will forever haunt me. "*The kraken!*"

Frozen in shock, we stayed rooted to the spot long after the unfortunate man's cry had faded into the still air around our ship—but one of us retained his composure. Captain Fox threw Arabella to the deck and dashed to the helm, his long hair streaming out behind him as he seized hold of the ship's wheel.

"Raise the ship!" he roared.

But as we leapt as one to obey his command and lift the *Eridanus* away from the ocean that would be our grave if we remained, the kraken—for that was truly what it was!—struck the ship again. We were now taking on water, but I was convinced that if only we could escape the waves we would survive.

With a shuddering creak, the *Eridanus* soared towards the sky; and for a glorious moment, I thought we had been spared. The captain's enraged roar told me the terrible truth of the matter.

The kraken's tentacles rose from the crashing waves to stretch towards us—and they were coming far faster than the vast ship could ascend.

I knew what I must do. I dashed to the lady's side and took hold of her hand. "Arabella, we must jump!" I urged her. "While the beast attacks the port side of the ship, we must leap overboard on the starboard side and pray we escape its notice."

She hesitated, glancing towards the captain as he paced back and forth, tearing at his hair in reckless abandon—and, to my relief, not sparing us even the swiftest of looks.

I touched her face. "Come with me," I said gently—and she, brave wonderful woman, did precisely that! We sprinted forward and leapt hand in hand as the beast attacked once more.

The kraken wrapped its probing tentacles around the hull in a loving embrace, and as we struck the water it snapped the *Eridanus* clean in two.

The crew, cargo and wreckage came crashing towards us in a flurry of flailing limbs and screams that rent the still sky above as we plummeted below the waves before we kicked out and broke back through the surface to fight for breath. Ensuring Arabella's survival and escape was my utmost priority, but I could not see how to achieve it—not only was the triumphant kraken still twisting and churning the ocean around us, but the captain himself had caught sight of her in my arms.

He battled through the chaos that had once been the *Eridanus* to swim towards us, gaining ground with every passing moment. Arabella cried out and clung to me as my keen eyes alighted upon the one thing that now could spare us.

The captain's remarkable flying contraption sailed upon the waves. Hope burst forth where moments before there had been none. I struck out with all my might, one arm still around Arabella for fear of losing her in the water, and a sudden gust of wind brought the leather harness directly to the sure grasp of my free hand.

She realised my intent and assisted me with trembling fingers to pull it on before taking hold of me once more. We could only pray that the clockwork engine had been made to withstand the water it had taken on.

It had.

We flew into the sun with Captain Fox's incandescent bellows and threats echoing in our wake. He could not touch us now, and he knew that just as surely as we did. Greenland was ahead. We soared towards it, free of the shackles he had placed upon us both.

VI

A month has now passed, and Arabella is asleep in our bed on board the *HMS Minuet* where we have booked passage together back to England. It was upon her urging I sat down to chronicle the terrors thrust upon us on board the *Eridanus*; she believed it would be a cathartic experience for us both to relive and recount them. The process exhausted her and I cannot bring myself to awaken her to share its completion with her; she has not been herself today.

Whilst we were on deck earlier, something troubled her. She spoke somewhat incoherently of a shadow passing across the sun that stole all the colour from her face and brought a fear back to her eyes I had hoped never to see there again. I brought her back to our cabin, and mercifully she seemed far calmer once I had done so.

But I understand what it is you want to know, dear reader. What of Captain Judson Fox?

We survived against the odds; there can be no logical reason to assume that he did not. To dwell on that would destroy us both with fear, though, so we have resolved to think no further of him. The writing of this journal is intended to put him from our minds once and forever—and on that note, I intend to write no more of him.

The sea is calm tonight. We are not alone on the still waters; I see another ship through the small window of our cabin. It draws near—too near! Good God!

~

(Publisher's note) Here the hand changes; Julian's fiancée, Arabella, takes over the narrative.

~

Julian has bidden me to act as his scribe and faithfully record the events now befalling the *HMS Minuet*. I am bitterly afraid and I fear I will not be able to write with as much clarity as he has done before me, but I shall do my best.

When he left off, the ship had been struck by a cannonball that smashed through her starboard side. He did not recognise the vessel that so inexplicably fired upon us, but the sight of the *Eridanus* is one that will always haunt me. Even in the dark I knew my captain's ship, and though all the laws of nature dictate she could not possibly be whole once more, she sails the sea before us as if the kraken's ravage of her hull had never happened. But then the *Eridanus* is no ordinary ship, and my captain is no ordinary man.

Julian has secured the door in the hope that we will escape their notice and be allowed to leave on the damaged ship, but I am afraid I am not so optimistic. This year's events have taught me how foolish it is to ever expect a happy ending. This is no coincidence.

Here is it; a sharp knock upon the cabin door!

My beloved has armed himself with what paltry weapons we have at our disposal in the cabin, but I anticipate we will find ourselves helpless in the face of the rogue that has come for us. If this journal must act as our legacy, then I fully intend to describe and name the terror that took us; for I know who is coming.

I have known since I saw him flying along the horizon in search of me earlier today.

It was always too much to hope he would let me go.

I hear it once more. I hear my name, crooned by the dark voice that haunts me.

This time, I know it is not merely a memory. He is on the other side of our door, raining down blows upon it to tear through the barrier protecting me from him even as he continues to call my name.

And through the now splintered door, I see the embodiment of the spectre that has stalked both my waking and sleeping hours for far too long now.

I see *him*—and I know he has come for me.

The captain has come to cage his little bird once more.

~

(Publisher's note) Here the hand changes back. Julian Ashton briefly resumes his narrative.

~

They say a dead man tells no lies. If that is so, then you, dear reader, can assure yourself that every one of the words you have read is true. I am a dead man, and this is my tale.

I am—was—a man of science and rationale. I held no stock in whispers of the paranormal, yet the events that tonight ended my life can only be explained as such. I witnessed the destruction of the *Eridanus* at the behest of the kraken, yet tonight she fired upon us and wrested my fiancée back into the arms of her villainous captain; a captain I am now convinced is as unnatural as his ship.

I can only hope fate is kind to Arabella and she will soon win her freedom from the renewed grasp of her oppressor. Even death would be a release, for then we would be reunited where Captain Fox would be unable to touch us.

My time draws near. The pull is too strong to defy much longer; I have lingered against all odds to finish our tale in the hope this journal will fall into the hands of someone able to discern the truth of the matter. My broken, bloodied body lies discarded on the floor of the cabin some six feet away from where I write this, and the *HMS Minuet* can be no more than a few moments from breaking apart. My last act is to finish this journal and seal it to await the hands and eyes of the living—a class

I can no longer count myself a member of.

Godspeed to it and may He have mercy on our souls.

~

(Publisher's note) The wreckage of the HMS Minuet washed up on the northern coast of Norway little less than a month after Julian Ashton's dated entry in his journal which finished here. The journal quoted verbatim above was in a corked bottle and discovered half a mile down the coast from the battered figurehead of the sunken ship.

Of Arabella and the Eridanus, there has as yet been no trace.

~

Skarett's Treasure

by K. R. Smith

Many a young lad romanticizes about a life upon the sea, but I must tell you, it is not all salt air and sea shanties; there is much hard work to it. Danger waits with every crest of a wave—from storms, the Royal Navy—which tends to look down on the likes of freebooters, and most of all, from your own shipmates. Put a bit of gold—or a fair maid—between two of them and there is a fair chance one will end up dead.

Not that dying is the worst that could happen to a man. Despite the unpleasantness of it all, as far as I can surmise you must only do it once. Sadly, however, I speak from experience on this matter, and although not entirely certain as to whether the cause is my desire for gold or for the company of a fine woman, it would seem that both have hastened my transition to this sorry state of affairs.

I received my first—and nearly last—taste of the sea while accompanying my master, Lord Jeffries being his name and title, on a journey to the Caribbean to secure trading contracts, not that there was much choice in the matter upon my part. I, Thomas Moreland, being but nineteen years of age and already in more debt than a man should have in a lifetime, had lowered myself to the lot of indentured servant through my ineptitude at gambling, or more specifically, at winning. A slight distinction I must confess, though nonetheless significant.

The point of it all was that his Lordship was hoping to initiate a business transporting sugar, molasses, and rum back from the colonies. My job was to make certain he looked presentable and carry whatever needed to be carried to wherever he travelled, all the while not complaining lest I get the back of his hand across my face.

We left London on a dreary August day in the year of our Lord 1698, passing out of the channel south along the coast of Portugal, skirting the northwest shores of Africa, then, only a few weeks out of port, bearing west with a steady wind at our back, into the open ocean.

My time during the crossing with neither trace of land nor bird in the air was both tiresome and frightening. There were long days under the sun when it was stifling below deck, and still, starless nights when the crew watched St. Elmo's fire dance around the mast tops, an ominous sign as ever one might see. Still, I found it quite the adventure, and hoped for further excitement whilst in the islands. To this, I must add that one should always be careful about what one wishes.

It was when we were but days out from our first port of call when our captain became rather distressed at the worsening conditions. The skies following the ship had darkened, and the swells seemed to grow with each passing hour. The wind increased to such a degree that the order to shorten sail was issued. It was in the early hours of the next morning when the storm caught up to our vessel, bringing with it a furious gale unlike any I believed possible.

As the storm intensified, those of us not part of the crew remained in our quarters as they fought to keep the ship afloat. Eventually, however, the relentless pounding of the swells washing over the boat took its toll and destroyed much of the rigging and the rudder. It was on the second night of the storm when our damaged vessel, floating like a cork in a maelstrom, struck a reef off the point of an island and began to go down.

At that time, Lord Jeffries explained how my duty was to him only; I should do whatever was required to prevent his demise and bear away whatever of his possessions he deemed necessary. Fortunately, his Lordship did not need to worry over the indignities of drowning as a length of wood came down upon his pampered skull—perhaps two or three times, although I seemed to have lost count in my enthusiasm—relieving him of that and of any other concerns. This was my chance for escape to a new life far away from any lords or masters.

I lowered myself into the water, making my way to a piece of yard floating by, and holding on as best I could, began paddling toward the island. The waves, breaking from all directions, made any progress difficult. Only the stark flashes of lightning casting their eerie glow upon the shore allowed me to gain my bearings. The last thing I recall was feeling something under my feet, whether it was the reef or sand, I cannot say, but I recall my body feeling very heavy and near exhaustion, with more rain than waves pelting my skin.

***

When I came to, she was there with a cup full of some medicinal brew, holding it to my lips, saying only the word "drink" with a voice that would make an angel jealous. I did not know it yet, but her name was Maria—Maria De Loma in full, and she was the sort of woman a man hopes to see when waking in a strange bed. She had dark eyes and dark hair that curled around her face like smoke from an oily fire, the same fire that was in her touch as she lifted my weary head upright, my senses overwhelmed by the haunting fragrance of warm spice about her body. She was the most exquisite woman I had ever beheld, and it would not have mattered if that cup held the finest whiskey or boiling lead, once she looked into my eyes, I had no will to refuse. After managing a few sips, Maria told me to rest. I do not know if it was her, my weakened state, or the drink, but I departed for the land of nod quick as a wink.

As it turned out, I was in a room—Maria's room—over a public house known as The Grotto located on the island of Tortola, some short distance from the main population to afford the privacy those in the profession of piracy desired. The establishment was a gathering place for the local men of the sea, and a place where anything, or anyone, might be available for purchase. To call it a tavern would be kind. Of the many young ladies employed there, the majority served something a bit more wicked than rum.

Maria was different, of course. While she did work in the tavern, she was also the equivalent of a physician for those seafarers, which would explain the many powders and potions she kept. It would also be the reason I ended up under her care. As I regained strength and became more keenly aware of the tenderness afforded me, I made every effort to extend the length of my recovery for as long as possible. Not that I believed Maria minded, as we had many long discussions during that time upon the state of affairs of my new island home and how one might escape its dubious charms.

While every moment I spent in Maria's company was memorable, I shall never forget the day when a local gentleman of the sea, Captain Skarett, arrived at her door. He was a large man, perhaps forty years of age and yet still quite fit, with a face full of graying beard that fell below his collar, and darting eyes that always appeared from behind a squint. He had come for a salve to help heal a wound on his leg, no doubt obtained as the result of his usual and customary business practices. As she worked to prepare the curative, Maria asked how long he would be in port.

"Not sure," he said gruffly. "I'm having a bit of trouble getting a crew together. A few too many seemed to have succumbed to the effects of our last encounter with Her Majesty's cannon. I need men who have been to sea, but I've a hunch I'll be taking anything that can walk."

"Why don't you take Thomas," she said, her accent making my simple name sound so wonderfully exotic.

The offer of my services came as a surprise, leastwise to me, though my recovery at this point was essentially complete and it was time for me to find some means to assist Maria financially for the treatment of my injuries.

"The boy?" Skarett asked.

"Why not? Even you had to start somewhere."

Skarett looked at me and said, "Can you handle a cutlass?"

"Well…"

"Have you ever even held a cutlass?"

I hesitated for a moment before answering, "No."

"Can you climb rigging?"

"I don't do well at heights, sir."

"Cook? Carpenter?"

I just shook my head.

"Thought as much."

I glanced over at Maria, feeling quite embarrassed, and apologized.

Skarett paced for a moment, stroked his beard, then said, "Be at the docks at sunup. I'll find something for you to do. My ship's the *Moondancer*, if you didn't already know. Just ask. Anyone can point the way."

With that, and a fresh bottle of salve, he was off.

Maria turned to me and smiled, and that was all I needed to know.

The next rising sun found me at the ship, and if I had known how soon adventure would find me, I might have decided against it.

It was on my very first voyage we attacked a heavily armed frigate. There was much cannon fire before we were able to board her, at which point chaos reigned.

Doing my best to avoid any participation in the conflict, I made my way along the rail toward the rear of the ship, hoping to find a spot to wait out the encounter. While stepping over several bodies, I found a cutlass no longer required by its previous owner, and thinking it a better weapon than the belaying pin I held, picked it up. A rather large and surly fellow noticed this, who then advanced upon me, sword raised over his head, and appearing as though possessed by the Devil himself. Not versed in the use of a sword, all I could do was hold the damned thing out in front of me. Who would have thought the fool would run right into the blade, impaling himself all the way to the hilt? He stood there, briefly displaying an unfortunate expression before falling to the ground, never uttering so much as a word. A few of the crew—and Skarett—looked over as he slid off my blade, and for that reason, and no other, assumed I had actually cut the brute down in a fair fight. Once the hostilities were over, both captain and crew accepted me as one of their own, a brave and hearty sailor ready to plunder the seas. I, of course, allowed them believe it.

As was the custom, each member of the crew received some portion of the spoils. The Captain got three shares, while those corresponding to officers received one and a half shares, and the rest of us, a single share.

Once back at the island, I returned to Maria, making a pleasing offer to her in the way gold and silver coins. She sat next to me holding her finger under my chin as if she was about to give me a kiss, and said, "You know, with enough gold, we could go to Spain, or perhaps Italy, and enjoy a comfortable life there." I never did get the kiss, but it was all I could do to keep my wits about me. Maria was like that, and she knew it.

Not a month passed before we were out to sea again, dodging in and out amongst the Leeward Islands hoping to find a merchant vessel, but with nothing to show for our efforts. Our luck changed when we sailed around a point on the east end of Dog Island to find a ship moving slowly to the northwest. Although we could not make out any flag, it was definitely a vessel for transporting goods, and not heavily armed. The rigging seemed to have suffered damage, which was the cause of her sluggish demeanour.

Our cannons were loaded with chain-shot in an attempt to destroy the remainder of the rigging, though the aim of our first rounds were less than optimal, tearing across the deck instead of through the sails. While not the intent, the result was as desired. A member of the boat's crew frantically waved a white cloth, allowing for no mistake of their intentions.

Skarett, still wary, approached for boarding with caution, cannons at the ready. Once on board, however, the reason for their surrender was plain enough. The port side, which had been facing away from us, showed heavy damage by cannon fire, with several gaping holes just above the waterline hastily repaired with tar, canvas, and wood in an effort to keep the ship afloat. The craft was in no condition to fight or flee. Other remnants of their previous battle were also plainly evident, with the stain of blood upon the decks and the few survivors of the original crew bearing wounds.

The captain of the injured ship had been cut in pieces by our low-flying chain-shot, with his top half on the main deck and legs still leaning against the rail of the quarterdeck above, a patch of crimson connecting the separate parts. Skarett stood over his upper portion, declaring he did not recognize the man, though in all honesty, I doubt his own mother would have been successful.

Those now manning the ship were from a privateer's crew that had seized the boat and were hoping to sail it in for repair or salvage. That crew had already removed any valuables to their own long departed ship, much of which had consisted of rum. Although a bit late to the party, Skarett decided to check the ship anyway, assigning me with two others the task of performing a search. Clarke and Whitlock proceeded toward the main cargo hold and fo'c'sle while I made my way to the rear of the ship and the officer's quarters.

My initial inspection confirmed little of worth remained aboard. It was when I became curious about the contents of a bookshelf that events took a turn. I noticed two volumes of ship's logs sticking out from an otherwise orderly arrangement, and moved to push them back into place. Though I attempted to do so, they refused to budge. I suppose my work for Lord Jeffries caused this to be an irritation to me, so I pulled the books out to determine the problem. That was when I found the sack.

The sack was nothing special, just tan cloth with a leather drawstring, perhaps hidden there hurriedly during the first attack. I could feel it contained some small items and was quite heavy for its size. As I untied the drawstring, I expected to find a few coins, perhaps a watch or minor pieces of jewelry, but what emptied into my hand was more than I dreamed, with cut and polished stones of good size, being diamonds, rubies, and emeralds, clear and flawless to my eye, and a few gold coins that paled in value to the other contents.

My first thought was of Maria, as this would surely be adequate to allow us to live in comfort, even in Italy. There was a problem, however. While gold was easily divisible for small transactions, large jewels were not, and selling them, having no trustworthy contacts within the islands, would be troublesome. I had no choice but to confide in Captain Skarett, and hope I might get a good share for my work. I heard Skarett speaking near the doorway, and called to him.

"What would be the problem, boy? Did you get lost?"

"I may have found something of interest—if we could speak privately."

Skarett seemed irritated at my request, yet entered the cabin, shutting the door behind. I said not a word, but shook a few of the jewels into my hand. His expression changed instantly, in awe of the colored stones in my palm. He held the largest up to the light, an emerald of the deepest green, and I watched the color dance across his face.

"We need to keep this between us, lad. These are no ordinary jewels. These are the sort destined for royalty. We'll not be able to sell them easily hereabouts, not for a fair price."

"How can we hide them from the crew?" I asked.

"Put them in a sling around your arm. Tell them you were cut on a nail."

"But there is no wound. What if they become suspicious?"

He grabbed my arm, pulled out a small dagger, and poked it with the point before I could pull back.

"That should be convincing enough," he said as the blood trickled down my sleeve.

Although not pleased with the method, it would provide an excuse for the sling. I wrapped my arm lightly, and then made a sling out of a large cloth from the bunk. Placing the sack within the sling, I held it tightly lest the stones make any noise.

Having made our apologies to the late captain, we departed the crippled ship, allowing the vessel and her small crew to pass without further molestation to whatever fate might await them.

Once back aboard the *Moondancer*, Skarett placed the jewels in the relative security of his cabin, and we discussed our options.

"We need a place to hide these where the others won't look," Skarett declared. "Can't leave them back at The Grotto. Too many prying eyes."

"Where might you suggest, Captain?"

"I think I know of a suitable place. Just to the east of town, maybe half a league, there's a small fishing village. Can't be more than five houses. One of them is a blue shack where a big black fellow lives. Meet me there the morning after we dock in Tortola—as close to sunup as those young bones of yours can drag themselves away from Maria."

"We're going to hide the jewels there?"

"Never mind that now. Just be there."

***

That dawn found me climbing into a fishing skiff with Skarett, a shovel, some canteens of water, and, of course, the treasure. We raised the small, triangular sail, gliding slowly around the point with the light morning air, and east along the island. After about an hour, Skarett steered the craft into a cove that contained neither house nor dock, beaching the boat on a small stretch of sand. The land, covered in dense foliage, rose sharply not far from the shore. Skarett jumped out and tied a line to a tree that grew conveniently close to the water.

As I disembarked, Skarett handed me the shovel and said, "Here. You can carry this. And the canteens. And, as a show of trust, I'll even let you carry the treasure."

"What will you be carrying?"

"These two pistols," he replied with a look that made me understand that I should not question him further. "Now follow me."

We walked a short distance along the shore, the Captain inspecting small indentations in the undergrowth, as if looking for something. As we continued, he began to explain his plan.

"There's an old church up the hill. The locals don't go there anymore—they think it's haunted. The way the damned thing looks, maybe it is. Anyways, it's nearly fallen down, but as I remember, there's a good spot nearby."

I looked up to where he pointed, which seemed more like a small mountain than a hill. I think the heat of the day had much to do with my temperament.

Eventually, Skarett found a narrow, overgrown trail that coursed through the jungle. It appeared to have once been a road, having narrowed from disuse. Although the first hundred yards were pleasant enough, it soon began to ascend the hill making the journey particularly disagreeable in the tropical sun.

As we trudged upward, my mind was on Maria as much as the treasure. Uncertain of my share, and if it would be enough to live well in Italy or Spain, I began to think of ways to increase my lot without Skarett being the wiser. Maria had told me once, "If you ever get hold of something good, keep it close to you." I always thought she was referring to herself, and perhaps she was, but the words seemed to echo with significance.

With Skarett ahead of me, he could not see as I reached into the sack withdrawing one of the jewels. I held it up to the sun, watching the light dance through the facets, sparkling like a star. I was nearly lost in its beauty when Skarett began to turn around. I had no time to return it to the bag, and if he thought I was stealing, there was no doubt he would test the edge of his blade on my throat. I stuck the stone into my mouth and rubbed my face as if to wipe the sweat away.

"Hot enough today, ain't it lad?"

I mumbled a reply while holding the stone in the back of my mouth, hoping he was not in the mood for a lengthy conversation.

"Well, not to worry. We've a ways to go, but most of the hard climb is behind us."

With that, he gave me a hard slap on the back, and the stone passed over my tongue and now rested within my stomach. I am unsure of the expression I presented at that moment, as Skarett gave me a puzzled look, but his thoughts soon returned to the matter at hand, laughed a bit, and resumed walking up the path. At first, I had a sense of fear, but reassured myself that he would never miss one stone. How could he? We had never counted them.

Maria's words about keeping close whatever good came my way returned. I wondered how much that stone floating around amongst my entrails was worth, and began to consider adding to the sum. Eventually, I pulled another stone from the bag and sent it on its way to join the first. Though not a tasty morsel, it was extremely satisfying.

I had soon managed to put over a dozen of the stones into safekeeping, and began to worry that the sack might feel too light or appear reduced in size. I knew I had to put something back in to make up the difference. If Skarett had a hunch on where the stones had gone, the method I envisioned he might use to retrieve his property was unsettling.

As we stopped to rest, I grabbed a handful of pebbles and stuck them into my pocket. Once the journey resumed, I took a goodly number out which corresponded roughly in size to the stones now resting within me and placed them quietly into the pouch.

Still, Maria filled my mind, and with each recollection of her jewel-like eyes irreversibly altering my plans, another stone travelled across my lips, with a similar pebble taking its place within the sack. I only hoped I did not begin to make noises from the stones as my stomach was beginning to feel uncomfortably full. I dared not even try the largest stone fearing it might not be able to pass through my gullet. I had no urge to die slowly of strangulation.

It was at this time I dropped a couple of the gold pieces down my boot, being careful to watch that old Skarett kept his nose going up the hill. My idea now was to make off shortly after hiding whatever was left of the jewels, with Maria of course, and leave the Captain thinking he had the treasure all to himself. The specific details of the plan were still uncertain. The few pieces of gold would help until the jewels once again saw the light of day, and I did pray for God's assistance they would not all reappear at the same time.

When we finally reached the church, it was just as Skarett described. Most of the roof was gone and little paint remained on what still stood. In truth, it would not be difficult to believe that the spirits of the dearly departed might find this a welcoming spot. Off to one side of the old church, a low, stone structure existed, built into the side of the hill.

"Ah!" Skarett cried out. "That'd be the place I seek!"

"Would a building such as this not be the first place one might search?"

He turned to me with a wide grin and spoke, "Not many men go into a crypt willingly."

The stones in my stomach seemed to grow in size with the words he spoke.

The entrance to the crypt was through an iron gate that had no lock, only a latch. Considering the contents of the structure and the local superstitions, any additional form of security would be redundant. Skarett lifted the latch and shoved hard against the gate, taking several tries to gain entry as the salt air and lack of lubrication had made the hinges rather tight. Once inside, there were a few steps down into a room lighted only by the glow from the entrance. Along the wall, a single candle sat on a shelf, and after cutting back the top to get a fresh bit of wick, and more than a few matches, the Captain managed to get it burning, albeit with minimal effect.

Although the back of the room had many alcoves that ostensibly held remains, the important figures of the church were in separate stone vaults standing in the middle of the floor. There were four of these, all covered with dust and mossy growths. Skarett looked around, and then brought the candle over to one that read, "Fray Francisco Vazquez."

"This is where we'll hide the goods until we can find a proper buyer. I want a secure place since it may take some time to find a man willing to deal with these sorts of stones. Put down the shovel and bag, and help me move this lid over some."

"We're putting the jewels in there?"

"Aye, lad. Would most men look in there if they didn't have to?"

"Probably not."

"Good enough. Now help me push this slab."

The slab was of cut stone, nearly three inches thick, and too heavy for one man to move. Skarett was a big fellow by all measures and would do most of the work, but even he needed help. As we pushed, the stone made an awful scrapping noise, enough to wake the dead I feared, and this sort of desecration made my tortured stomach even more uncomfortable.

After much effort, the lid was finally moved enough to place the sack within the vault. I picked it up and started to put it inside when Skarett rested his hand upon my shoulder.

"Before we put the jewels into their hiding place, let me see some of that treasure one more time."

I cannot tell you how nauseous I felt at that moment, wondering if before the day was over this crypt might have another guest. I reached into the bag, feeling for the large stone that I could not swallow and the one piece of gold I thought still remained. With the dimness of the light inside the morbid structure, it was difficult for Skarett to view the contents of the pouch, though my fingers were able to discern the treasure from the pebbles. I pulled them out, holding the large emerald next to the candle, its light splayed across the crypt in the most beautiful exhibition the inside of that horrid edifice had ever witnessed. Even in the shadows, I could see a smile on Skarett's face.

"Make sure you put the sack under the body—just in case."

"Under the body?" I asked in disbelief.

"If someone should take a look in there, I don't want it sticking out in the open."

"What sort of person would even consider doing such a thing?"

Skarett stared at me, his eyes glistening in the candlelight, and spoke quite slowly, "People like us. Put it under the body."

For that insinuation, I hid the remaining two bits of treasure in my palm while appearing to replace them in the sack, then positioned the bag of pebbles as requested.

I wish to note that there is something quite disconcerting about inserting one's hand amongst the rotting and decaying remains of another person, even a member of the church. With the miserable job completed, I dropped the stone and gold piece into my pocket and wiped my hands on my trousers. After where they had been, I was grateful there were no more stones remaining that would require my fingers to be near my mouth.

We returned the stone slab to its original position over the vault and set the candle back onto the shelf. Once Skarett touched the wick with his fingers to extinguish the flame, darkness again filled the chamber. Upon exiting to the world of the living, the Captain used his weight to pull the corroded gate shut, set the latch, and then took a brief last look inside.

Apparently satisfied, he turned to me and said, "Bring your shovel. We have one more job to do."

I had originally assumed the shovel was to dig a suitable place in which to bury the treasure, but since that was obviously not the case, I was curious as to what the next job was to be. I followed Skarett down the path a good distance until he took a turn directly into the brush. He said nothing, but glanced back and forth as if hunting for something. Finally, he came to a stop in a small clearing surrounded by saplings and brush.

"This is where the hole should be dug."

"Here? Why?"

"Aye, here!" he grunted, waving his arm over the spot. "There is more treasure yet to hide," he said with a wink.

"More treasure? How will you ever find this place again? There are no good landmarks—only bushes and a few small trees, and no sightlines to any hills or houses."

"Trust me lad," he said with squinty-eyed nod. This fine spot will be as good as any."

We stood the for a moment, with me looking over the area trying to figure out why he wanted a hole dug in this particular location and Skarett standing with his fists on his hips and an displeased expression upon his face.

"So, dig the damn hole," he commanded. "A big one, big enough for a chest that could hold all the gold in your dreams," he laughed.

For the life of me, I could not imagine what treasure it might be, and the thought of dragging a large chest up the hill seemed to be an impossible task. Moreover, I had serious misgivings concerning my ability to swallow even a single additional stone, let alone an entire chest of riches.

"What sort of treasure might this be for?" I asked, desiring to delay my work as long as possible. "Gold? More jewels?"

"In time, lad. In time. Now just dig."

After clearing away a bit of undergrowth, I reluctantly stuck the blade of the shovel into the red earth and began lifting the dirt away, sweating profusely in the bright sun, and realizing that being a captain meant you did not do the work, but merely watched as others performed your bidding. As far as digging was concerned, it was a wonderful place. The soil was soft and light, full of worms and insects scurrying about, all trying to hide from the commotion I was creating. Still, there seemed to be neither rhyme nor reason to the location.

After shovelling for some considerable length of time, I asked if the hole was large enough, but the Captain, upon inspection, declared it far too small for the intended purpose. This process continued until the hole was so deep that I could not easily climb out, and nearly as wide in all directions. Exhausted and confused, I asked once again, "Will this do?"

Skarett looked it over and smiled, "Aye, lad. That will do nicely. Hand me your shovel and I'll help you out."

I passed the shovel up to Skarett and then remarked, "I suppose we have to get the treasure now."

"It's already here."

"What? There's no treasure here," I insisted, turning to view the empty cavity in which I stood. "All I see is the damned hole I've spent most of the afternoon excavating."

Before I could turn around, I heard the hum of something moving quickly through the air, and then felt a sharp pain in my head just before all went dark. Had I been lucid, this would be the moment I realized that

I had not been the only one with a plan to obtain an increased share of the booty. I also might have worried that Skarett knew the true location of the jewels.

After a short while, I came to, in a manner of speaking, as little was clear to my eyes. The humming sound I had heard was the shovel coming down upon my own skull, based upon the blood still on the spade and the pain coursing through my brain. Skarett was now using that same shovel to push the soil back on top of me. If I had have known this earlier, I would have tossed the thing into the ocean. He could see I was still alive, but that seemed to be of minor consequence. I thought he might have discovered that I held the treasure within, but his words, and the location of my grave, told me he had no idea he was hiding the jewels in a place he would never again be able to find.

"Sorry, lad, but it's hard enough for one man to keep a secret, let alone two, and what you know of that crypt is as valuable as the treasure itself."

He kept shovelling, each measure of soil landing on my battered body making it more difficult to breathe, hiding the daylight from my eyes, until finally I could see and breathe no more. At least the aching in my head went away.

That was the last time I saw Skarett, or anything else for that matter. Nor shall any see me again as the trees and vines of this steamy jungle quickly cover my final resting place, my earthly remains forever hidden. True, the events of my life did not turn out as I had wished, what with myself becoming prematurely deceased. It also appears that any plans I had for Maria will now be quite impossible, the thought of which truly is worse than death. Though out-witting the Captain, I gained nothing for my efforts. Indeed, I am much worse off. The Captain had also out-witted me, but will eventually realize the cost of doing so when he returns for his jewels. It would appear that dear, sweet Maria is the only person to come out of this unscathed, as her charms will easily allow her to find a new conspirator in her efforts to escape the pirate islands. Still, I must admit to some sense of superiority inasmuch as the Captain is concerned. For as of now, and perhaps always, only I know the hiding place of Skarett's treasure.

Lips

by Stephanie Ellis

Lips smile; lips kiss; lips laugh. Lips curl; lips sneer; lips kill. What other use can lips be put to? Perhaps I might think of something and let you know, for the moment though I am busy. I have company, and I must not neglect my guest.

Already the sweat is running in rivulets down his face. His eyes are full of anger and … something more. Yes, there is definitely more there. I see it flitting about, a glimmer, a sliver, a shiver of fear.

He sits alone, the terrible Captain Ned Lowe, abandoned by his crew and left to the fate that I, judge, jury, and probably executioner, decide. But I forget my manners. It is only polite to introduce oneself. I know enough of society to know that. My name is Captain Luis Alvares. My ship is, or rather was, the *Nostra Signoria de Victoria*, one of the finest schooners in the Portuguese fleet. Her captaincy has been my reward for the many successful voyages that I had made. Whether for trade, transport or exploration, I performed my duties diligently and efficiently. Until I ran into Ned Lowe, I had never had much of a problem with pirates either.

Of course I had heard the stories, how he tortured his prisoners on a whim: decapitation, disembowelment, you name it, he did it. A particularly nasty trick of his was to bind a prisoner's hands and weave the rope between the fingers. The rope would then be lit and allowed to burn through the skin, eating away at the flesh until it reached bone. Their screams, it was said, drove Lowe into an even greater frenzy. By the time it was my misfortune to cross his path, even his crew had begun to doubt his sanity.

The events of that day have been seared into my memory. You're probably thinking that I too had my hands bound and burned, but my suffering was to be more extreme, only a few of my crew lost their hands. Should I take pride in that? I don't know.

***

It had been such a good voyage up to that point. The skies were clear. We had a fair wind, and we were on our way home with 11,000 gold *moidores* in my safe. The hands were in high spirits, eagerly looking forward to their wages, and the women and grog that'd buy on reaching port. Their dreams were of a safe harbour and a warm bed. Then came the cry from above.

"Ship ahoy!"

I was not too concerned at that point, not until my first mate Rodrigues came running up to me. Even beneath the tan of his weather-beaten face, I could see his face had paled. I frowned—he was not a man to scare easily and that worried me.

"Captain. The flag sir." he said.

"You've identified her?"

"Aye. She's a buccaneer sir. Red skeleton on black."

He didn't say more. He didn't need to. The word had spread amongst the men. Already they were making preparations to outrun the ship. I lifted my spyglass and fixed on our would-be assailant. I was under no illusion as to our fate should we be caught.

The Fancy—without a doubt. Two men stood on the quarter-deck, one of whom I immediately recognised as the infamous Lowe. Whilst I had never seen the man before, his description had been widely circulated. One look at his face, at the mockery of a mouth scarred by some accident, and I knew it was him. If we could outrun him, we would be safe.

Our luck, which had held for so long, chose that moment to fail us. The wind dropped, and made us sitting ducks. The devil himself must have been steering Lowe's ship for still it came on, bearing down on us with terrifying speed. Then I decided that whilst Lowe might take my ship, he would not get my gold.

"Mister Lopes!" I called.

"Aye, Captain."

"With me to my cabin."

We made our way below decks to my cabin where I had stored the gold in my safe. Lopes found a canvas bag, sturdy enough to hold the coins. Together we filled the bag, and then Lopes tied it to a rope so it was able to hang safely outside my cabin window. Should need arise I would be able to cut the rope and send it down into the deeps; should we be successful, I would be able to haul it back in.

The battle, which I will not describe here, for the memory is too painful to a man of my rank, was soon over. The decks were slick with blood, and my men, what remained of them, were crammed into the hold. Our attackers took me to what previously had been my cabin to await Lowe's pleasure. It was with some satisfaction, even when I thought my death was imminent, to see the frayed rope that dangled from an open window.

When Lowe looked up from my desk, my stomach lurched and it was with difficulty that I managed to retain my composure. A jagged slit ran from both sides of his mouth and up to each ear, carving a permanent smile into the skin. A botched attempt at stitching the wound meant that his mouth never closed properly and when he spoke the muscle and tendon beneath his cheek was exposed. I swallowed hard, trying to force down the bile that had risen in my throat. Yet, despite the horror of his face, I refused to look away.

I do not remember the exact moment that the pirate discovered my subterfuge. One of his men approached him, somewhat hesitantly, and said something in a low voice.

Lowe initially said nothing but it was as if the atmosphere in the room had charged, just like before a storm you could sense something building. The crew avoided looking at each other, avoided looking at their captain. His fist sent the poor messenger flying across the room and then he turned his blazing eyes on me, glowering with a rage that only confirmed my growing dread.

"You denied me my prize," Lowe roared. "The gold is mine by right of conquest!"

Terrified, I somehow managed to look him in the eye. Whatever I said would not change what I knew was to come. If I had known *how* he intended to finish me, perhaps, I would have kept quiet.

"There you are wrong sir," I replied. "That gold was the result of honest trade, of the toil and sweat of my men. I will not allow it to be soiled by your hands. Better it be sent to Davey Jones."

His fist found purchase in my gut and sent me sprawling to the ground. Rough hands seized my person. Blood and humiliating tears mingled in my eyes, blurring my vision. Shame burned my cheeks as they dragged me back up on deck to be paraded in front of the rest of his men.

But just as swiftly as the storm had come so did it pass. Lowe surveyed me, calm once more, much as one gentleman does another when introduced for the first time. Despite my own suffering, I could not miss the nervous glances of those of his crew who now stood by him; nor did it escape me that those on the edges of my vision had surreptitiously moved themselves a bit further into the background. The small time I had been allowed to observe him had given me a chance to recognise the sudden calmness as the first sign of the madness that followed.

Yet still, I was merely apprehensive, when in fact, I should have been terrified.

"So Captain, you will not hand over the gold," Lowe said, amiably enough I thought. "Sometimes I find that good food, good wine, can be more persuasive to bringing about a certain meeting of minds—don't you think?"

Still that smile, but I had my standards. "That depends on the circumstances, sir. Amongst gentlemen, such an outcome can be envisaged, however, I do not believe that I am amongst honourable men. Therefore I am afraid, I must decline your offer."

Lowe's smile remained, fixed into that terrible grin of his, a smile that did not reach his eyes. "Oh, that is a pity but I must insist that you at least dine with me, Captain. The law of hospitality demands it. In fact, I take great pleasure in offering you the *choicest* cuts. I doubt you will find you have ever tasted better."

He called his cook forward, a burly sweaty man who did not seem to care for the niceties of personal cleanliness; unlike the pride I found he was to take in the care of the tools of his trade.

"Your knife," Lowe demanded of the man. Reluctantly, the implement was handed over.

The pirate approached me, still smiling, the knife gleaming in his hand. A chair appeared and I was rudely invited to take a seat. A table was placed in front of me. Another order was given, and a small makeshift stove was prepared. A greasy looking broth soon simmered nearby. Somewhat bewildered, I peered up at Lowe as he towered over me. I searched his face for answers but could find nothing. Slowly, the conviction grew that I was looking into the eyes of a madman

"You will not allow your lips to talk," he said. "Lips that do not talk are useless. I think a little food for thought may encourage you."

Lowe came closer, forcing me to see my reflection in the ruthless blade that he held, almost lovingly, in his hand. Gently, he allowed the knife to caress my cheek. A tenderness, a lightness of touch, that I had not expected. Then came the pain, such pain as I have never experienced. He took his time, cutting slowly, carefully, the agony becoming even more unbearable with each incision. My vision blurred and warm rivers of blood flowed freely from my mouth. My screams seemed to come from some place far away. Through the misty film over my eyes, I watched in horror as the pirate threw my flesh into the pot, wishing unconsciousness would claim me. My face burnt with pain as I waited for whatever other torture he had in store for me.

I expected to be carved up, a feast for his men; there had been rumours of cannibalism in some of the stories that had reached my ears. Instead Lowe took a bowl and ladled the disgusting concoction into it, slamming it down in front of me so that its greasy droplets sprayed my face. He filled a spoon and thrust it into my hand.

"Eat," he ordered.

I stared down at what had once been a part of me. Those lips of mine which had once commanded, had tasted, had kissed and finally, had defied, swam in front of me.

"Eat" ordered Lowe again, this time holding the point of the dagger to my throat.

My hand trembled violently as I guided the spoon towards the remnants of my poor mouth. The bile rose in my throat, and I had to fight the nausea to prevent myself from gagging.

"Eat," roared Lowe, losing all patience and forcing the spoon between my jaws. He clamped my mouth shut to prevent me spitting out its contents.

I could not chew. This was unclean, ungodly. I choked. Struggling and gasping I found another mouthful being forced on me. And another, and another. I could not breathe. I could not see. I prayed that my ordeal would soon be over and that death would claim me, and so the darkness came, took me to another world where spirits walked, seeking their revenge.

***

Now the Captain is my guest, at my table. A table for one. I have kept the broth simmering for a long time. I have seasoned it with the suffering that he has inflicted, the pain he has caused. The salt comes from the tears of the innocent, spiced with the anger of the murdered, peppered with cries for justice. The stock that is the blood of his victims now boils with their anger.

"Cook," he bellows into the darkness, furious his meal is late. Lowe does not know I have driven the servants from his house although I think that he senses he is—almost—alone.

I conjure up a fire in the hearth. Its light explodes across the rooms, fiery tendrils writhing around Lowe's seated figure. He turns towards the source of the heat; its intensity making him sweat. I watch as he notices the cauldron. Still he sits; he does not run.

I pick up the knife. Its movement hypnotizing him as it floats ever nearer. Its sharpness reflected tenfold by the fire. Still he sits; he does not run.

Then he speaks. "They say I am mad, and so I must be if I see a knife before me but no hand to hold it. If I am mad then this is not real, just pretty illusion—that is all." He smiles.

I pour him a cup of wine which he drinks without comment. The knife I move closer, closer, until it is kissing his lips. Now it is I who smile as I carve his flesh, laugh as I toss the extra ingredient into the pot. He screams now.

I put a bowl beneath him to catch the blood that drips down, the fear he sweats out. All this I will add to the pot. Now he tries to run, but I do not let him. I? I should say we, all those he has wronged in life now place their hands on him, forcing him down. So still he sits; he cannot run.

I fill a bowl, a generous portion, and place it in front of him. Solicitously I select one of the choicest cuts and spear it with a fork. I let him savour the aroma, that heady smell of revenge … of death. Then I invite him to taste, ignore his aversion, push the meat between his teeth. He chokes. Other ghostly hands join in.

We feed him forkful after forkful, spoonful after spoonful, until even the bitter dregs have been swallowed and the pot lies empty. He sits quietly now, no breath, no movement. Lowe has eaten his last meal and dined well. We clear the table, as all good hosts do and leave our guest, appetites sated.

Lips smile; lips kiss; lips kill.

The Regular

by A.P. Sessler

It had been an hour since Sandy gave the last call at the Ships' Grave Tavern, a centuries-old favorite since the British occupation, found on the southern beaches of North Carolina's Outer Banks. The added-on dining area that seated about 50 served decent sandwiches and fresh seafood, but the tavern's real draw was the historical bar that managed to survive every war on Carolina soil, the Prohibition and the Great Depression.

It also had its own ghost stories, which superstitious drunks would frequently recite (or rewrite) on an especially chilly or foggy evening, such as the one in progress.

Sandy, herself a favorite of locals, was in her mid-20s. The busty blond frequented the tanning salon in the cold off-seasons to maintain her bronze summer skin for those sunrise jogs on the beach—it didn't hurt tips either when she wore her tight, black v-neck shirt with the tavern's logo in white.

The thirsty crowd present that evening gradually thinned out until not a glass was left standing on the bar except the giant margarita glass filled with cash. The bar wasn't officially closed; however, until Sandy killed the power to the televisions on either end and the stereo system beneath. She emptied the tip glass and counted the cash before pocketing it. It was a good night. She proceeded to clean the bar for the morning shift, starting with the sink full of dishes.

Sandy repeatedly wiped the stubborn lipstick on the rim of a glass. It squeaked and squealed as she ran the wet dish rag back and forth across its surface, the lips opening wider in a distorted smudge as if they were about to speak.

Someone cleared their throat.

Sandy swung around startled, finding a customer seated at the bar. She dropped the lipstick-stained glass onto the floor, shattering it to pieces.

"Jesus, you scared me!" she yelled with her hand over her pounding heart.

"The good Lord, I'm not, but thirsty, I am," said the man. "I'm apologizing for scaring you out of your wits, and for being the cause for your broken dish."

"It's all right," she said, pausing to catch her breath. "I couldn't get the lipstick off anyway."

When her heart quit racing she retrieved the broom and dustpan. As she leaned over to sweep the broken glass into the dustpan, the gold cross necklace she wore swung back and forth. It caught the ceiling lights and sent their reflection across the room.

"That's a fine necklace," he said.

"Thank you."

"Might I inquire how it came into your possession?"

"My grandmother gave it to me," she answered. She leaned the broom against the counter, then glanced at the man. "I've never seen you before."

"'Tis the only place I drink," he assured her.

"You must come on my off nights."

"That or you come on mine," he quipped.

She emptied the dustpan into a bucket half-full of broken glass from the night's dropped dishes, then put the broom and dustpan in a corner cranny. As she casually slid the tip glass closer to the man, she took a better look at him.

He had a red faded t-shirt with some illegible text on it, underneath a worn leather jacket. Tattoos extended beneath the jacket's cuffs and ended at his wrists. His face had deep creases where every muscle met, yet it only lent to his masculine beauty. His gray-streaked black black hair ran through a silver braid and ended in a ponytail.

"I'll need to see your ID," she said.

"I'm begging your pardon."

"Your identification," she clarified. "Your driver's license?"

He sifted through his pockets in search of the requested item. "I'm afraid I must have misplaced it."

"I can't serve you if you don't have your ID."

"Is such a trivial thing truly of import to you?"

"I could lose my job if you're working for the ABC."

"You mean to say the government?" he laughed.

"Yes, I mean the government."

"Do I look like I work for the government?"

"A lot more than the teenagers they send in do."

"Sending children to do a man's job? Now that be dirty!"

"So if you don't mind, I will have to see your ID."

"Madam," he said impatiently, "I have as much respect for the current government as I do for a wharf rat. They take what they want and make sure the rest is fit for nothing."

She looked from side to side suspiciously as she contemplated the consequence. "I'll serve you one drink, but I swear if you pull a badge on me I'm gonna kick you where it hurts so hard you'll never walk straight again!"

"Madam, one thing I do value are my stones. That I'd never lie about."

He had a quick wit. It made her smile.

"So what would you like tonight?" she asked.

"I be in the mood for something different."

"How different? You don't look like a fruity drink kind of guy to me."

"Give me whatever you be partial to."

"How about Sex on the Beach, or a Buttery Nipple?"

The man blushed. "A lady should never be so forward," he advised.

"I don't name the drinks, I just make them."

"Just a word of wisdom: Only a seaman should swear like a seaman."

"What? Oh! You mean ladies shouldn't cuss like a sailor. I try not to cuss but sometimes I get so mad it just slips out."

"I understand. Some of us are only—"

"Human?" she interrupted.

"That were the word I be looking for."

"Okay, then," she said as she mentally went over the drink menu, "how about something not so vulgar?"

"That would do well," he smiled.

"I think I have the right drink in mind for you," she said confidently.

"Oh? And what be that?" he asked.

"I'll surprise you."

After ringing the drink in on the computer she prepared and and served it.

"This I like," he said, then took another sip and swished it in his mouth before swallowing. "'Tis very agreeable to the palette. How is it called?" he asked.

"A Blackbeard."

"Pray tell, why did you assume it was befitting me?"

"I like the way you speak. You sound like a pirate," she said.

"I be not a pirate," he said as his eyes darted nervously about the bar with his back hunched low.

"You are too funny!" she said with a laugh.

"I be not jesting."

"You need to take it easy. It's just the name of the drink."

"Very well, then," he said as he sat up straight, suddenly confident. "Now if you be partial to pirates, I do have tales to tell."

"What kind of tales?"

"All manner, but my favorite be the tale of a phantom pirate who haunts this here tavern," he said mysteriously.

"Oh, please!" she rolled her eyes. "Whatever you do just don't tell me the one about Tom Olde. I've heard it so many times and so many different ways I'm sick of it!"

"I'll wager you've not heard mine," he argued.

"I doubt it. I've heard them all. Like the one where his spirit kills people outside the bar because British soldiers wouldn't let him come in, and the one where his spirit follows waitresses outside and rapes them so they'll bear him a child to carry on his name.

"I've also heard the one where he comes into the bar looking for his stolen treasure and kills anyone wearing jewelry. I even know the rhyme for that one. 'Tom Olde had locks of gold.' I never got what having blond hair had to do with him killing people. Oh, and let's see, lastly there's the silly one where his spirit gets really hammered and thinks he's aboard his ship, so he starts giving orders to all the customers—that's the one I would really like to see."

"'Tis absolutely wretched, the whole lot of it!" he said as he turned his head and pouted in a near childish tantrum.

"See? I've heard them all."

"But alas," he disagreed, "your ears have yet to hear my tale."

She went to the computer and rang in another drink, then prepared it. "If you can tell me one I've never heard before, this drink's on me," she said as she slid the glass in front of him.

"See, Tom Olde *was* a pirate, in that the stories agree," he started. "But he wasn't so merciless a cutthroat he spent his entirety pillaging, pilfering, plundering and killing. He had as soft of a soft spot for the ladies a man of the sea can have. That, and for the ale of this tavern, of course. So once in a blue moon when the fog rolled in and made it difficult for a sailing man to weather the stormy sea, he would set anchor just offshore this island.

"He insisted his men drink their fill, until not a soul aboard could lay one foot before the other. Then, with the fog as his cover and knowing the British couldn't see past their own bayonets, he'd take a lifeboat ashore all by his lonesome. He'd lay in wait for some suspecting soul coming or going, then subdue him just to borrow his clothing for a spell so's he could enter unawares to the British soldiers who were wont to frequent this here establishment.

"Once inside he would partake as many a privilege as an honest citizen could enjoy. Of course in those days it was unheard of for a woman to man the bar, so he spent his hours at yonder a table, just to lay his eyes on any maiden willing to attend his needs. He always left a happier man than went he came. 'Tis why to this day he still returns to this tavern from time to time, just to lay his eyes upon a buxom beauty."

When he finished his story he downed the drink and placed the empty glass on the bar proudly in anticipation of her response.

"I'm sorry, but that's the lamest ghost story I've ever heard in my entire life," she said. "You owe me for that one."

"Why?" he asked. "Has it been told to you?"

"No," she said.

"Then the bill is yours. You mentioned not that the story be good, just one unheard."

"Okay, but you better tip good," she said as she reached into her pocket for her tip money. She hit the SALE button on the cash register and placed six dollars in the drawer.

"Why do you fault my tale?" he asked.

"What ghost would haunt a bar of all places just to look at a hot girl? Aren't ghosts supposed to find their peace and move on?"

"I know nothing of a girl with fever, but I assure you it's the proper tale. Now this moving on which you speak, what more could a soul ask than to spend eternity partaking what he delights in most?"

"What about Heaven? Doesn't a ghost want to go to Heaven?"

"Not all souls are fit for such a place. And who knows that those who are, aren't allowed from time to time to wander the earth, since it and the fullness thereof are the Lord's?"

"That's too deep for me. I just know that I've been tending here four years and I've never heard or seen a thing."

"Well, 'tis a tale after all. Now what say one more drink?" he asked.

"Another Blackbeard?" she asked.

"If you will," he said.

She rang in another drink and set it before him. He slowly drank it then reached into the back pocket of his blue jeans for his black leather wallet. He fingered through several bills until he found a ten and a five-dollar bill.

"Will this suffice?" he asked as he handed the two bills to her.

"Sure will," she said. She hit the SALE button on the cash register. Its chime resonated through the old tavern's woodwork. "Give me just a second and I'll get your change."

"None required," he smiled.

"Thank you," she smiled back. His tip wasn't the greatest but it was still 25 percent.

She printed out the register's service report, then counted the money. As she leaned over in front of a large safe below the counter and unlocked it to place the paperwork and money inside, the gold cross of her necklace again fell out and sent its reflection across the room. A brilliant white cross shone upon the man's face.

"I once had more wealth than you can imagine," he said as he stared at the light that danced along the walls. His eyes followed the reflections to their source.

"Really?" she asked.

"I was the victim of robbery," he explained with his forlorn stare fixated on her as she closed the safe.

"I'm sorry," she said.

"So am I."

"All right," she said as she stood up from the safe. "It's closing time, so sorry, but I'll have to ask you to leave now."

"You mean to say you're here alone?"

"Since we're a small business the owner lets bartenders close shop to avoid paying extra labor, just as long as the cash and paperwork are correct."

"It doesn't seem just, leaving a beauty as yourself by her lonesome. I hope it seem not strange if I request the favor of seeing you on your way."

"Normally I wouldn't because there are a lot of creeps around here that try to pick me up, but you seem sweet," she said with a smile.

She took her purse from the bottom shelf and put it over her shoulder. When she came from behind the bar he took her arm in his. She tried to pull her arm away but soon found his other hand resting upon her elbow.

"Don't worry," he said, then smiled. "I won't be *picking* you up."

She laughed nervously as they approached the entrance. When they reached the door he stood still in the shaft of moonlight coming through its small window. The silver light reflected convex crescents on the edge of his dark eyes in profile. He seemed to be in a trance, mesmerized by the moon, as if listening intently to a voice.

She stared at him, just as speechless and still, until she saw the lump of his neck lower and rise as he swallowed.

"Shall we?" he asked stoically, still facing forward.

She swallowed herself, unsure what awaited beyond the doors. The fluttering butterflies in her stomach bid her onward, and she followed them freely.

He held the door open as the two exited.

"I have to lock up," she said, silently requesting to be released from his grasp.

He let go of her arm so she could lock the door. She took the keys from her purse, purposing to keep her arm free but as it rested just for a moment on the door handle he found an opening to secure it again within his own.

They stood on the gray-painted railed plank walkway outside the tavern. The thick, low fog that hovered just above the ground made visibility minimal.

"Would you look at that?" her voice trembled as she forced a smile. "I won't be able to see 10 feet in front of me. I'll have to drive slower than a turtle."

"The marsh has taken many a traveler in weather like this no matter their pace," he cautioned her.

He took a long look at her car. "Your vessel is quite peculiar. I imagine it be fast."

"It's no Corvette but it gets me where I need to go."

A smile carved its way back into his rugged features. "A Corvette—

now there's a vessel to my liking. I imagine it took some wealth to procure your vessel" he said as he stared at the gold cross around her neck.

"I don't know about that. It just means I went in debt for 10 years."

She noticed there was only one vehicle in the parking lot.

"Did you walk here?"

"That I did."

"Do you need a ride back to where you're staying?"

"That won't be necessary," he answered, still gazing at the cross around her neck. "But before I leave, satisfaction must be met."

With their arms still locked, he reached his free hand into an inside pocket at his side and retrieved something. She saw a momentary glimmer of light. He held his closed fist just under their locked arms and hesitated. Unable to pull her arm from his strong grasp, she reluctantly reached with her free hand and took hold of his.

When she felt his fingers slowly open, she opened hers ready to take whatever he brandished. She felt a cold metal edge against the flesh of her palm. Her eyes blinked involuntarily and her mouth went dry. When she closed her fingers upon the metal she felt its dimensions. It was perfectly round and quite obviously just a coin. Having worked in the service industry for a decade she could tell the value of any coin by size alone. She was certain it was a John F. Kennedy half-dollar.

She was instantly relieved to know if wasn't the murderous knife she imagined in the back of her mind. She swallowed her pride and pretended to be grateful. "Thank you," she said.

"I'd give you more, but I do have to spend the remainder of my fortune sparingly."

"I understand. Times are tight," she said as she quoted the same line given to her from those who stiffed her on too many occasions.

"That is the truth to be certain," he agreed.

When they reached the small stair at the corner end of the walkway and descended to the bottom step, he stopped. Her feet were on the gravel parking lot, while his barely hung an inch over the last plank step.

"I'm afraid this is as far as I can take you," he said.

"I would be too forward if I wanted you to take me further," she said flirtatiously.

He laughed as his face turned red. "You've made this old soul blush twice now."

"You know, I do work here almost every night. Maybe you could come by and see me again."

"I wish I could for you've been so tolerant of me, but truth be told you'll only see me once in a blue moon," he said as he gazed at the moon and made a sweeping motion with his hand. "But, before I take my leave I wanted to tell you the proper rhyme. 'Twas not 'Tom Olde had locks of gold.' It were 'Tom Olde had lots of gold.' At least he used to."

A cold night's gust blew his gray-striped locks to one side along with her golden hair. Their long hair became entangled in the strange wind. He stared into her eyes as his body transformed into spirit and then faded into the color of the night air. Without flesh and bone to support them, the clothes he wore crumpled into a heap.

The strong arm that was locked with hers became a phantom limb. The leather jacket sleeve collapsed under the weight of her arm until his clothes clung to her legs. Sandy screamed as she looked down at the jacket arms that held her. She pulled her legs free of the sleeves' grip and ran up the steps and along the side of the tavern to the end of the handicapped ramp.

At the end of the ramp there was a man's body laid flat on the ground. The mounted light from the nearby telephone pole revealed only his pale bare legs protruding from behind the back wall. Sandy's breaths became short and staggered as she slowly turned the corner to see who the victim was. The upper half of his body was hidden in shadow.

Sandy used her cell phone to shed light on the fallen subject. There were long tattoos running the length of both the man's arms just like the phantom in the bar had. Her heart started to beat faster. When she followed each arm to its wrist she found the man had nothing on him but a pair of boxers, a pack of cigarettes in one hand and a lighter in the other. Her eyes followed the light from his torso up to his bald head and saw his face was turned away from her. He had a bloody gash on the top rear of his skull with dried streams of blood running front and back. She leaned over the man to see his face. It was Johnny, one of the bar's regulars. She screamed at the sight of his limp body.

She started to dial 9-1-1 when she heard a ghastly moan, then a low, deep voice.

"Sandy," the voice spoke.

She aimed the cell phone light back at Johnny. He didn't move an inch.

"Johnny?" she asked fearfully. "Was that you?"

He slowly turned his head to face her. When he saw the cell phone light he covered his eyes. "Get that thing out of my face, will ya?"

"Oh God, Johnny! Thank God, you're alive!"

She ran back to the pile of clothes the phantom had worn and returned with them. "I thought these looked familiar," she said.

She laid the clothes down at his feet then took the cigarettes and lighter from him. "Hurry up and put them on," she ordered.

As he sat up, the rest of his body was illuminated by the telephone pole light. "If I find out who did this I swear I'll kill him," he said.

"I think someone beat you to it. That was Tom Olde."

"Get outta here! I've been coming to this place for 10 years and I've never seen or heard a thing!" he said as he zipped his pants.

"That's why you're half naked with a cut on your head. Now come on, get your shirt and jacket on. It's cold out here and I'm scared he might come back," she said through chattering teeth. Her fear made the damp, frigid air even colder. It burrowed into her bones and made her shiver all over.

"Did he hurt you?" he asked, taking his lighter and cigarettes from her.

"No. I just don't want to see any more ghosts tonight, okay?"

As Johnny pulled his shirt over his head, Sandy placed her hands in her pockets to warm them. She had rather been in the still warm bar than outside, but being next to a live man of Johnny's size seemed safer, even if he was only flesh and blood.

Her fingertips brushed against the coin Tom Olde gave her. She removed it and held it above her head until it eclipsed the full moon completely from her sight. She turned the coin from side to side while her other arm was folded over her chest. The parking lot lights reflected across the coin's surface back and forth.

Johnny had just finished donning his leather jacket when he saw the gleam of light from the coin. He squinted his eyes tight to focus. He asked, "Is that—"

"I think it's gold," she interrupted.

Johnny shook his head then firmly massaged his left temple with his fingers before taking a second, clearer look. "That's not just gold, that's a Spanish doubloon," he declared. "He really was here!"

"I already told you that. Now please, Johnny, can we go inside?"

"All right, all right. I heard you the first time," he said. He started to stand, but his wobbling knees wouldn't cooperate. "Can you give me a hand?" he asked.

She tucked the doubloon between her breasts for safe keeping, then bent down and put an arm around Johnny's back, and he an arm around hers. She helped him to his feet and up the plank walkway until they came to the entrance. Johnny leaned against the wall next to a window while she fumbled through her purse for the keys.

When she opened the door she helped the regular inside then immediately locked the door behind them.

"What do you want? It's on the house," she said as she stepped behind the bar.

"I couldn't do that," he said, rubbing the back of his head.

"You kinda already did. Tom used your wallet. I can't refund the money now since it's on the paper but you can have whatever you want."

"What did Tom drink?"

"Three Blackbeards."

"Figures," he laughed. "I'll take the same."

"You sure?"

"You only live once, right?"

"Unless you're a ghost."

After she crafted his drink she poured herself a shot of bourbon.

"To Tom Olde," toasted Johnny. "Who hits as hard as he dies."

"To Tom Olde," she said, then downed the shot as Johnny gulped down his drink in large swallows.

The two drank until the sun rose and dispelled the phantoms of that peculiar night—the kind that comes only once in a blue moon, when the fog rolls in and makes it difficult for a sailing man to weather the stormy sea.

The Engine Room
by Alex Douglas-Mann

The flames made me think of hell. The burning was the worst pain I'd ever felt. The brightness of the coals around me was unbearable until my eyes fried and withered in their sockets. I opened my mouth to scream, but my throat and lungs burnt away from the inside out.

It can't have lasted more than a couple of seconds no matter how long it felt, and any sound I did make would have been covered by the roaring of the furnace.

***

The Age of Sail is dead. I used to say it blew away. Either people didn't understand the joke or they didn't think it was funny. I was the only one to ever laugh.

Now, we have to fight fire with fire. Almost literally, but not quite. If whoever you're chasing isn't relying on the wind then you can't either, which means a steam ship. And a steam ship means a furnace. And that's where I ended up.

The problem with piracy, whether independent or under a letter of marque, is that it doesn't attract the best people. I wasn't the best either. I killed and stole with the rest of them but I'd hoped there'd be some honour amongst us despite the saying.

Not that it matters. I'm here now. Bill, who mans the engine, throws coal in for me and I burn brightly on. When the door is open I can see into the engine room itself, and when Bill brushes his shovel against me I can feel it. I'm warming to Bill. If I could laugh at that I would.

***

There isn't much for me to do in here. I'm getting a feel for the ship. I can sense the paddles and, if I try really hard, I can flare myself up. Bill gets confused when this happens.

I spend most of my time trying to work out which of the cunts on board dumped me here in the first place, but being stuck in the engine hampers my investigation. I can hear the rest of the ship. There's the creaking of wood and the splashing of the waves, but if I concentrate I can hear the voices too. It's easier when Bill has stoked me up. If I'm left unattended too long I get lethargic.

I thought I'd listen at my bunk to see if I could hear anybody going through my things when they knew I was past caring but no such luck. Instead, the lot of them piled in and shared it out when they realised I wasn't coming back. None of them bothered to ask where I'd gone. No accusations and no admissions.

I live, or exist, in fear of missing something important. A tell-tale comment. I can't listen to everybody, just a single conversation at a time, and how do I know which is the one that will set me on the right path? Johnson slamming his cleaver into the last of our rancid meat stores? Mason dangling from the rigging like a fucking monkey? They're all murderers. That's why they're here.

So I began to come up with a list of suspects. Bill is an obvious choice as he's got access to the furnace at all hours, but I can't bring myself to really suspect him. Each time he opens the door and I see his shovel wobbling towards me I feel a little thrill. Not you, Bill, you didn't kill me.

Out of everybody else on board I can only think of three who'd bear me any kind of grudge. There's Simms, who lost a bollock when he tried to fuck me one night and discovered I sleep with a knife; Wise, who dislikes me for God knows why but will try and start a fight with me whenever he's drunk; and Jones, who thinks I'm a waste of space and would rather my share of our takings got split between the rest of them.

Other than them it could be anyone, but they're the only people I can think of with motivation, so they're who I'll listen to.

Apart from tuning in to Simms, Wise and Jones whenever I can, I spend my time eavesdropping around the ship half-heartedly, hoping somebody will say something that helps, but mostly just looking for interesting conversations. The best time is when everyone is eating in the galley and I can listen to them all at once. The worst is when people are asleep and the few who aren't barely talk. That's when I just ignore the outside and concentrate on the engine itself, flaring up or cooling down to control the speed of the paddles, reaching out to the flames that surround me and trying to twist them this way and that. Learning the limits of my new existence. Sometimes I listen to Bill snoring.

***

A week after my disappearance a fight breaks out on the main deck. The yelling reaches wherever I was listening before so I turn my attention there instead, as does everybody else. It sounds like there's a crowd already from the number of footfalls, with two people circling each other in the middle. I listen for the voices. Fights aren't rare. The day I was killed, Johnson cut off some of Davies' fingers when he caught him stealing food. Two weeks before that, Tyne, our captain, pulled out a revolver in a fist fight and shot Maggot in the head. He said the rules didn't apply to captains. We dumped the body overboard.

This time, one fighter is Jones. I've missed whatever the fight is about but it's begun now and there's not going to be any backing down. Somebody is going to be left badly beaten, if not dead, whilst the other... Well, they could end up the same way. I hear Jones rush forward and get knocked aside. A taunt is yelled. The other man is Wise. This could help me. If only I'd heard the start and knew why they were fighting.

Jones has picked himself up and charges again. The footfalls begin dropping together and become confused. I don't know who's winning, who's on top. There are cheers from the crew but I just want them to shut up. I need to concentrate.

My anger makes the furnace flare. The ship jolts as the paddles groan against their gears and then burst to life for a moment. Approaching footsteps mean Bill has noticed and come to see what's wrong, which calms me.

The fight is still going on. I can hear them rolling on the planks now, the occasional thump as a punch or a kick connects, a series of crunches when one of them has his head pounded into the tarred wood. A gagging, a choking, when one finds a loose bit of rigging and wraps it around the other's neck. That last sound goes on for a while. The crew have fallen silent.

Eventually, there's a thud as whoever's lifeless corpse is now on board hits the deck. I hear feet move away from it with a limp. The man starts swearing to himself as he walks. It's Jones. Wise is dead. I doubt anybody is surprised. Jones has always had a vicious streak and won't hesitate to take the upper hand when it's given to him. He won't hesitate to kill either, as Wise found out. Maybe Jones is my man.

Or not, because Simms is somewhere else. I can hear his tuneless whistling in the magazine, sensibly kept away from the furnace. The noise is faint but there. He must have heard the fight but he stayed where he was. Or he heard it and moved to the magazine knowing he wouldn't be found.

He's leaving now. His footfall walks away and the door shuts. I'd give anything for a pair of eyes to see what he's up to but I've got nothing to give anymore. Bill shovels more coal in and I take to brooding, thinking about what I know. What if Wise was the one who killed me and I'm now avenged? But what if he didn't and my killer is still roaming the ship. I need to carry on investigating.

Jones is now being bothered by Remy in the bunks. Remy could never tell when it was time to leave somebody alone, which is why I'm going to hear him shoved against a wall any second. And that's undoubtedly what that bang was.

I was never very nice to Remy, but nobody was nice to Remy. Remy got the worst jobs and the worst jibes and the worst beatings. Had a bad day? Hit Remy. Not want to man the furnace while Bill sleeps? Beat Remy until he did.

The only thing I remember Remy ever saying to me was that he liked my hair. He had a slow, drawling voice, but I don't know if it was always like that or it was because of the constant beatings. We weren't gentle with him. He got knocked unconscious more than must be healthy.

He liked my hair though. I miss my hair. It was good hair. Dark with tight curls. The sea air ruins some people's hair but mine thrived. On land it was boring. Flat and hanging off my head like limp, decaying seaweed. But on board it came alive. The wind and the salt and the moisture did something to it, like it had always meant to be at sea.

It doesn't matter now though. It's just ash at the bottom of the furnace, or maybe thrown overboard.

My teeth must still be somewhere too.

***

It's been another two weeks. Simms is dead. He had a secret stash he was keeping in the magazine, drink and money from what I heard. Somebody saw him heading in there one night, did some investigating of their own, found his stash in a barrel of gunpowder he must have emptied. They snitched on him and he got strapped to the deck and beaten a bit too vigorously. It happens. Nobody cared too much. I listened to them scrub the blood off the planks.

I'd been listening to him for most of that time. Whenever he opened his mouth he'd have some disgusting new side of his personality to put on display. If it was him that killed me then I'm glad he went out in such an undignified fashion. Even if he didn't, I can't muster any pity for him. He deserved more as far as I'm concerned. That's a problem in itself though. I still don't know if he did it or not and now he's dead. Three deaths in three weeks. This ship is going to shit.

It means I only have to keep my eye on Jones now but I'm starting to think it must have been Simms or Wise. Nothing Jones says or does makes me think it was him. I've even heard him talk about me to a few of the other crew. He still calls me a waste of space, but he said he'd beat to death the whoreson who killed me if he found out who it was. There were a few murmurs of agreement. Not many, but some.

It could all be a lie to throw people off the scent of course, but why would he bother?

It's frustrating. He's my last suspect and I'm losing my suspicion. What if it was Simms or Wise and I'll never know? What if it was somebody I hadn't even considered? They could just walk off at the next port and I'll be stuck in the fucking furnace never knowing. I can feel my anger building and the flames flaring, and I calm myself down before I work my way through the coal.

Bill has already noticed though. He walks over and opens the door. I light up the engine room as he peers in. He shakes his head and grabs the shovel. Sorry, Bill. I didn't mean to bother you.

The fresh coal gives me the energy to start listening around the ship again. I decide it's time to give up on Jones and start from scratch. It's upsetting but I don't have any other choice.

People are all over, all in different places doing different things. Where do I even begin? Alphabetically? By seniority? I have no idea. No fucking idea. Somebody is walking in down the stairs to the engine room. Whoever it is, they'll be as good a starting point as any.

Except it's Remy. It's fucking Remy. Sent down to see if Bill needs a hand, doubtless because somebody else got fed up of nursing him, having him underfoot, and how hard is it to shovel coal?

Too hard for Remy. Every time he's down here, he either smothers me or is too sparing. I just ignore it and wait for Bill to get back. He knows how to treat me.

Bill knows what a fuck-up Remy is too, but he reluctantly hands him the shovel. He needs to check some of the mechanisms above the furnace. I consciously simmer down so it's not too hot for him up there.

Normally, when he's shovelling, Remy is silent. The brain-dead prick probably can't concentrate on two things at once, but today he starts a conversation with Bill, yelling his slow, stuttering way over the sound of the engine. I like listening to Bill speak. He's calm and constant. I don't even pay attention to the words in his replies, just to the rhythm of his speech and how it seems to work around the creaking of the ship, the waves hitting the hull.

It really is strange. Each splash of water marks a syllable for Bill, but he doesn't speak slowly or sound odd. He just seems in tune with the ship. Every movement made to work with it. Step gently up and down the deck. Tweak what needs to be tweaked in just the right way. I start to wonder how long he's been on board to get each of his movements just right. It's then that Remy announces he killed me.

It takes a moment for me to realise what I've just heard. Bill might not even have been listening. I can still hear his spanner working somewhere above me but he doesn't reply, even though Remy definitely just confessed to my murder.

He carries on talking about it. How he pulled the bag over my head. How he was surprised by how much I struggled. What it smelt like when I was burning up. He'd even tested it with rats before he flung me in to make sure that the working of the heat would brittle the bones, ready to break into easily missed chunks after the ashes were forcefully raked.

He burnt away my hair. He's the one who has taken the little I had and turned it into ash and soot. And he's finally confessing to Bill, my Bill, who doesn't even fucking hear?

The best part, my favourite part, is why. Bill obviously isn't listening, but Remy tells him it's unlucky to have a woman on board. I'm nothing but dancing flame because of this superstitious cocksucker and I'm going to do something about it.

He's been laying the coal on heavy. It's smouldering in a big pile in the middle of the furnace. I've retreated to the edges to make sure he doesn't extinguish me with a badly placed shovel-load. Now, though, I dive into it and I burn as hot and as bright as I can. I feel air rush in through the open door as I use up the oxygen. The pile of coal ignites and I feel like I used to when we were storming a ship, revolvers indiscriminately tearing through wood, flesh, bone. Screams and shouts everywhere. The look of terror on a man's face when he turned around in time to see my gun flash straight into his eyes. I felt good. I felt strong. I felt powerful.

Remy brings the shovel into the furnace again. I grab it and pull with everything I can muster. It gets dragged into the flames. Remy looks surprised. Too surprised to let go, so he gets pulled forward as well. Everything feels like it slows down and I watch his forearms get closer and closer to me. At last, they're in reach. I grab them.

The sizzling begins before I've even wrapped myself around his wrists. I can see them smoking and hear his screams. The look on his face is more gratifying than anybody I've killed before. I pull again.

What I enjoy most is the way his skin seems to bubble slightly before it blackens. Once he is close enough I grab his torso, embracing him, engulfing him. I pull him into me. He tries to scream again but I fill his throat and lungs. I caress every part of him and watch as he collapses away. Even as the smoke and ash blow in the heat, I wrap flames around them too, just to be sure. I twist and crack his bones. I watch every single one of his hairs burn into nothing. I devour him like only fire can.

***

It felt like hours and I loved every minute, but it can't have lasted more than a few seconds. Now that Remy is gone and the coal burnt down, I stop dancing and look out. Bill has jumped down. His hands are blistered. I must have burnt him when I flared up. Sorry, Bill. He looks confused and then shuts the furnace door.

I'm alone again. It's not dark because I create my own light. I feel satisfied. I know that soon I will be given more coal. Soon I will chase another ship. Soon I will dance and flutter and sway in patterns only I can make sense of.

Buried With Treasure

by John Vicary

"Wakey wakey, eggs and bakey!"

Captain "Red Locks" Perrow tried to blink his eyelids to shut out the glare of the hot Caribbean sun and tell his subordinate he could shove his cutlass right up his own arse because he happened to be vegan—thank you very much—when he realized he didn't have any eyelids to blink. Damn. Was he still a corpse?

"Now, Captain, there's no need to panic. The situation is as follows: You're a corpse."

This isn't the first time I've been reanimated for profit, he tried to say, but all that came out was an extended "Uunnghh."

"That's just the lingering effects of the hoodoo. You'll be fine in a moment," the cheerful voice said. "Uh, fine being a somewhat relative term, of course. No, I'm quite sure you'll be fine. Donny Knuckles over there has been reading up on witchcraft, and he assures me that everything is kosher so far. Wave, Donny, so the captain knows who you are."

The captain tried to focus on the pirate, but all he could see was a blur of motion. It was too damned bright without eyelids.

"Ah, it's all right. Plenty of time to get acquainted, I say. Now, sir, I realize you've been through a lot but there are some things I'd like to ask you—"

Captain Red Locks didn't know why he couldn't move his arms, but he did know what made everything better. "Get me rum!" he shouted, or something to that effect. Rum was a cure-all, even in death.

"Now, Captain, rum isn't going to help," the man said. "What I need to ask—"

"Rum certainly *will* help," Captain Red Locks said, pleased that his jaw responded at last. "Or at the very least a visor of some sort, because that sun is blasted bright. Why can't I move? And who are you to be speaking to *me?*"

The man cleared his throat. "Er. I'm Roger Gribble, ship's accountant. You're a skull, sir. I thought we explained that a moment ago. Donny, you said he would retain information."

Donny Knuckles shrugged and opened his well-thumbed copy of *Hoodoo for Dummies*. "It says right here that he should be 'in the same mental state as he was when he was rendered deceased.' 'Snot my fault if he was a simpleton when he died."

"That's a metric ton of helpfulness, thanks, Donny. The point, sir, is that you *should* be able to comprehend that we've used magic to bring your corpse back to life to tell us the location of your legendary treasure," Roger said.

Captain Red Locks would have waved his arm around if he'd been in possession of one. "The last time I was zombified I had an actual *body*," he said. "This is a major downgrade. Also, I had the honor of speaking to the ship's captain, not some ruddy bean counter."

Roger nodded in sympathy. "I understand your disappointment, sir, I really do, but please try to realize that we're in a bit of a pinch here. Payroll issues and all. We simply didn't have the means to bring all of you back to life, so we—I—made an executive decision to bring back only the most necessary part. After all, you don't need your legs to tell us about your treasure, do you? Let's be logical. We're also in a bit of a jam with regards to timing here, so if you could be a dear and just tell us where you stashed the loot? That would be splendid."

"Don't remember," Captain Red Locks said, sticking out his bottom lip. Or he would have, if he'd had lips.

Roger frowned. "Come now, don't be like that. I'm sure you do remember quite well. The stories say you had the greatest treasure on the seven seas, but there's never been a single glimpse of it in all these long years since you died. Everyone has tried their hand at finding it, but no one has ever managed to discover where you hid it. Your horde has attained a mythical status, and a quest to locate it is almost a precept of modern-day piratical life. You can't forget something in as grand a tradition as that!"

"I can." Captain Red Locks sniffed. "I did."

Roger paced the deck. "What do you want in return for telling us the location? I'll give you anything. By 'anything' I hope you recognize I'm employing the use of hyperbole, and I really mean 'whatever falls within a reasonable rate of exchange', of course. I'm a man who calculates rate of return on investments in both simplified *and* compound interest for a living, so don't let's be silly."

A dull ache formed behind Captain Red Locks' superciliary crest (once he'd raided a vessel carrying a scientist, and he'd kept the pilfered chart of the anatomy of a human skull displayed in his quarters ever since) as he realized how much he disliked accountants. Times had, indeed, changed when actuaries made the deals rather than men of action. He thought through his list of demands. He'd been all over the world and seen everything there was to see—twice—and he'd been brought back to life, and even traveled with the circus for awhile as part of an aerial acrobatics troupe the first time he was a reanimated corpse. There wasn't anything this clerk could offer him that he hadn't already had. He was tired now and just wanted to be left alone. "You must promise to re-bury me with a part of my treasure so that I can be left forever in peace. And also get me some kind of sunglasses, because I'm getting a headache from the perpetual glare."

Roger thought for a moment. "Granted."

Captain Red Locks cleared his throat. "Then I will give you the first clue. We must go to the place where:

> My thunder comes before the lightning;
> My lightning comes before the clouds;
> My rain dries all the land it touches.
> What am I?"

"What sort of trickery is this?" Roger asked.

"I didn't keep maps," Captain Red Locks explained. "The way to my hideouts was always in my noggin." He would've tapped his head for emphasis, but he figured Roger got the gist even without his appendages for clarification. "Say, does anyone have any gum?"

The Quartermaster stepped forward and offered a stick. "It's just strawberry, sorry."

Captain Red Locks grimaced. "Hey, it's fine, really. Thanks, me heartie." He was nothing if not polite, after all.

"No problem."

Roger tapped his foot. "So can't you just tell us where this place *is?* I don't have time for all your nonsense. The timecards need to be balanced, you know. Have you ever had a mutiny because you can't pay for time and a half? It isn't pretty. So knock it off with the poetry and just tell us where the treasure is buried."

Captain Red Locks sniffed. "It isn't poetry. It's a riddle. And I can't remember; I always went by the verse."

Roger groaned. "But what does it *mean?*"

Captain Red Locks thought. "I don't know. It's amazing that I remembered that, to be honest. I can also recall my old footlocker combination, isn't that weird?"

"*So* weird," Roger agreed. "Are any of the crew good with riddles and the like?"

Blackjack Davy Duncan raised a hook-hand. "I am, Mr. Gribble. The mateys and I tell each other word games to pass the time on second watch, and that one's easy enough. I think Cap'n Red Locks is talking about a volcano."

"Yes! I am!" Captain Red Locks said. "It's all clear now. A volcano. Indeed." He blew a big pink bubble.

Roger blinked. "Well, which one? There are hundreds of volcanoes. We could sail for a month of Sundays and never find the right one!" Being excellent at math, he knew exactly how many days that was, and he didn't want to be stuck on the ship for even a fortnight of Sundays, if it came to that.

"Begging your pardon, sir, but it's easy to tell which one he meant," a sailor by the name of Knee-Biter McGillicuddy said. "See, if you know the geological activity of one-hundred fifty years ago, which would put us at old Captain Red Locks time ... no offense intended, sir."

"None taken," the captain said around another bubble. Age was largely only a number, he'd always felt, and he was about two hundred eight years young and counting.

"Anyway, if you match up the differences in active volcanic eruptions in the centuries, there are three dormant volcanoes for the entire region where Captain Red Locks was known to roam. Only one of those is on an island, the most likely place for a pirate's plunder, due to its relative inaccessibility for the general public. That puts us on the course straight to the Seaweed Cliffs," Knee-Biter said. Then he blushed, because he hated public speaking. It was why he'd gone into pirating work in the first place.

"The Seaweed Cliffs!" Captain Red Locks said. "I swore an oath never to return there!"

"What? Why?" asked Roger.

Captain Red Locks cracked his gum. "Oh, I just always wanted to say that. It sounds so dramatic, don't you agree?"

Roger began to look as if he was regretting the entire endeavour. "Tell the Sailing Master to chart a course for the Seaweed Cliffs," he said.

The crew settled into its routine of hauling ropes to hoist various sails, and the captain chomped on his wad of gum and relaxed as they cruised across the open ocean. A powder monkey finished his job of restocking the orlop and the allure of a talking skull proved too great a temptation to resist. He crept closer, examining the bone. "Is it true you were a famous captain from a long time ago?" he asked.

Red Locks forgot he couldn't nod without a neck, and he ended up just rattling himself on the deck. "The swashbuckliest," he said. "Captain Red Locks Perrow, at your service."

"I'm Nick Flint," the boy said. "Why do they call you Red Locks?"

"Well, I wanted to be Dreadnought, but it just wouldn't take," the captain said. "I had a deaf boatswain—sorry, 'hard-of-hearing', he was so sensitive about that!—and he was always saying "Red Locks, Red Locks" no matter how many times I corrected him. Also, I had curly red hair. But still, who wants to be known by a key trait of their physical appearance? It's like when the lads call you 'No-Legs Nick.'"

The boy stared. "No one calls me that. I was just born without legs."

"Fair point; My hair *was* gorgeous so it's hardly the same. Still, 'Dreadnought' had a lovely ring to it. I wish it would have caught on." Red Locks blew his wad of gum over the railing. It had lost the strawberry flavor a long time ago and now merely tasted like a mouthful of chewed-up erasers.

"I have some stuff to do." No-Legs Nick (as the captain was to think of him forevermore) inched away.

"Me, too," Red Locks said, trying to look busy. "Me too."

The ship sailed for a few hours, and a cry from the crow's nest signaled their arrival at the Seaweed Cliffs. Roger held him up to see the volcanic skyline. "We were serendipitously close to the Cliffs when we found your skull. We're almost there. Now what?"

The next part of the riddle popped right into his mind. "Clue the second:

> What always runs but never walks,
> often murmurs, never talks,
> has a bed but never sleeps,
> has a mouth but never eats?"

"That's a cinch!" Blackjack Davy said, waving his hook around in his excitement. "A river?"

"Of course!" Roger said. "Even I could have come up with that one. So, we follow the inland stream, is that the course?"

"I guess," Red Locks said.

Roger narrowed his gaze. "What do you mean, 'you guess?'"

"I dunno; it's just been a long time, you know? I always had a head more for words than for navigation. Funny how I ended up as captain of a whole crew of people with basically no practical skills to speak of, now that it comes to it." Captain Red Locks cleared his throat to break the somewhat uncomfortable silence. "No matter; we're here now! River, you say?"

"No, you nitwit! *You* said!" Roger shouted.

Red Locks looked around the fast-approaching isle. "Yeeesss. I'm sure it will be fine. The river. After all, who makes up a mapping-riddle and then doesn't follow the directions in the rhyme? Anyway, have you ever tried to come up with the correct rhyme for 'sleep'? It's devilishly difficult, I tell you. I couldn't think of one and in the end went with that near-rhyme of 'eat'. I hope no one noticed."

"Barkeep?" Roger asked.

"Dust heap?" Blackjack Davy said.

"Knee-deep?" Knee-Biter McGillicuddy suggested.

"Upsweep?" No-Legs Nick called from under decks.

"Little BoPeep?" said the erstwhile necromancer, Donny Knuckles.

"Phsaw, I say," Red Locks said. "As if kneedeep has anything whatsoever to do with a *river*. Come now."

The ship sailed around the treacherous Seaweed Cliffs and anchored in Rum Cove (a distressing misnomer, much to Red Locks' perpetual disappointment). A scouting party disembarked at the mouth of Cannibal Estuary (less a misnomer than Red Locks might have hoped) and made their soggy way up the Coconut River Valley.

After an hour of sloshing through the jungle, Roger pulled Red Locks' skull out of the pack in which they'd stashed him. "We've been walking for a long time. We're at the heart of the island. We have to be close. Where *is* it, damn you?"

Red Locks looked around. "This just isn't ringing any bells."

Roger shook him. "Think harder! We're at the edge of a fiscal cliff here. And an actual one, which is where your head is going if you can't remember where the booty is."

"Fine, fine. Clue the third:

> Whoever makes it, tells it not.
> Whoever takes it, knows it not.
> Whoever knows it, wants it not."

"Wait, that's the auditor's secret passcode!" Roger said. "The answer is counterfeit money. How did you infiltrate our order? Is there a mole in the Comptroller's Club? And more importantly, are you scamming us?" His hand shook with suppressed rage while the rest of the band of pirates looked on in horror and exhaustion (they were a bit out of shape to be tromping around a jungle proper, to be honest, though Donny Knuckles had a nice set of pecs going on).

Red Locks laughed. "No, just having a wee bit of fun with you. Sorry, I couldn't resist. Last clue, really:

> Reaching stiffly for the sky,
> I bare my fingers when it's cold.
> In warmth I wear an emerald glove,
> and in-between I dress in gold."

They all turned to look at Blackjack Davy, who scratched his head. "It's a tough one," he said, repeating the phrase. "Some kind of lady is all I can think. But I don't think it's right."

"Nope," Captain Red Locks said.

"Gloves when it's warm?" Knee-Biter asked. "I don't know. A statue of some kind?"

"Uh-uh."

They all had a turn guessing, but the riddle stumped them. Captain Red Locks grinned.

"Wait," Donny Knuckles said. "Do *you* know the answer?"

"It's a tree!" the captain shouted. He would have done a jig if he had feet. Only No-Legs Nick knew his pain.

Roger clapped a hand to his forehead. "Your clue led us to a tree in the middle of a jungle?"

The crew groaned.

"Of course I remember which one," Captain Red Locks said. "One that looks like a cloud. It seems I should've had a riddle for a cloud, but I don't. At any rate, it has a really weird shape. I'll know it when I see it."

"This was one hundred some-odd years ago!" Roger said. "The tree is probably dead; or worse, it wasn't real to begin with. Your memory's been scrambled since we revived you!"

"This was a fool's quest, Gribble!" Knee-Biter said. He grabbed Red Locks' skull and hefted it into the brush.

The captain's world tilted as he rolled over and over. He was glad not to have a stomach or he would've been sick all over himself; as it was, his gorge was fighting the good fight to rise up against him. He came to rest deep in the forest, and when his vision stopped whirling, he saw the canopy above him. The sheltering branches formed a familiar spiky green cloud. "Come quickly!" he yelled. "My treasure is here!"

The crew found him lodged in the roots of a dragon tree. Roger leaned over him. "You said something about treasure?"

Captain Red Locks didn't blink. "This is the spot. Under this very tree is my heart's greatest treasure."

"Look!" Blackjack Davy nudged at a spot of soil near the base of the tree. "There's an indentation … something is here!"

They unpacked their spades and began to dig (even Blackjack Davy, who had a difficult task shoveling what with his hook for a hand). They didn't stop their work, even when night fell. Donny Knuckles took a moment to light some candles to ward away the deepening gloom, but they continued to chip away until a scrape broke the rhythm. "I've hit something!" Knee-Biter said.

"Sounds like metal. Could it be a chest?" asked Blackjack Davy.

"Get down and see!" said Roger.

They knelt around the hole and lifted a weather box from the dirt.

"Is there more?" Roger asked. "That's a rather small chest to contain the world's greatest treasure."

"It is just the size it needs to be," Captain Red Locks assured them.

Knee-Biter held his shovel to the rusted lock, and it gave way almost instantly. "This is it," Roger said, as he lifted the creaking lid of the little box. Donny Knuckles shoved a candle forward and they all peered together with a collective intake of breath.

A second later there was a mass recoil. "It smells!"

Blackjack Davy waved a hand in front of his nose. "What's that stench?"

"It's a rotten corpse of some vermin!" Roger said. "Explain yourself, Captain!"

Captain Red Locks didn't have an endocrine system anymore, but he felt a rush of adrenaline as if he did. "With pleasure! You've made a fatal error, good sirs. That isn't vermin; that's my trusty parrot, Treasure!"

"Say what?" Donny Knuckles asked (he always had been a bit of a colloquialist).

"What I mean to say is that my beloved parrot, appellated Treasure, was stricken with some form of avine ailment and was carried off this mortal coil to fly in the clear skies of heaven," Captain Red Locks said. "Besides the fact that a pirate without his parrot is a laughingstock, I realized that the greatest treasure lies not in doubloons or in earthly wealth, but in family, the kind I was denied with the departure of my dearest Treasure. I spent my remaining years telling everyone of my secret, that I had found the greatest treasure a man can find: love."

Roger sank to his knees. "Are you kidding me?"

Blackjack Davy snickered. "He was in love with a bird!"

"Not *in* love … but indeed I did love him. And he loved me. Treasure was my boon companion, the only thing in this world I could trust," the captain said.

Blackjack rolled on the ground, tears of laughter streaming from his eyes.

"Shut up, you idiot! It isn't funny!" shouted Roger. "Don't you understand? We've been following the ravings of a lunatic for over a century!"

"Oh. I probably should have mentioned that he had a reputation for this sort of thing," Knee-Biter said. "They called him Lead Rocks Perrow, since everyone knew he was apeshit crazy at the end there. They suspect it was lead poisoning from the make-up he used to paint his face."

"I *was* a bit of a dandy," Red Locks admitted.

"Yeah, always on about one crazy thing or another. In fact, he was so saturated with lead by the end that I'll bet even his skull is steeped in the stuff. We'd better not touch it anymore," Knee-Biter advised. "Best just … cut our losses. I don't know about you guys, but I'd rather die of scurvy like a respectable pirate."

"Fine. Let's go," said Donny Knuckles.

"Wait, what about the mutiny?" asked Roger, trembling. "There's no money now, and Tuesday is a pirate holiday. I can't afford to pay out double time!"

"It's fine, Roger," Knee-Biter said. "We knew this was a bit of a side-trek. We found old Captain Red Locks Perrow's treasure, though, and that's bragging rights! No need to specify what it is to folks, exactly. We just gained a bunch of sea cred. We can hang on until the next big score."

Roger nodded. "Thanks, guys. The captain will be pleased with your loyalty. He's sure to crack into his store of rum to reward you. Let's go."

"Wait!" Red Locks said. "You promised to re-bury me with the treasure. Don't welsh on a deal, now. I held up my end, now you do your part."

Blackjack Davy sighed. "He has a point. It'll only take a minute."

"You'll take the spell off, right?" Red Locks asked. "I mean, no one wants to be underground for all ti—" He was interrupted when he was thrown into the chest, and the lid slammed shut, leaving him in complete darkness. There was some tilting as if he were being lowered into the ground, then he could hear soft mounds of dirt piling onto his new grave. The stench of rotting bird feathers was still quite pungent, but being with Treasure's remains didn't bother the captain. He didn't have the glare of that burning sun in his eyes anymore, and he could sing all the shanties he liked. His new home suited him to perfection. He let himself grin and started his song. "One hundred bottles of beer on the wall…"

Yes, he was going to like it here.

Dead Men's Tales' Contributors

Mellissa Black (editor) is a small town southern girl, but since graduating high school has lived across the U.S. and now lives in Northern Alabama. She is a graduate of Limestone College with a B.S. in Computer Science and is pursuing her Masters in English from the University of Alabama in Huntsville. Most of her stories are set in the South and the colloquialisms of her youth always shine through. When she's not writing or working on her studies, she enjoys spending time with her two children and two fur babies. Find more by visiting: http://terminalsunshine.com.

Kevin R McNally is an award-winning actor. Born in the hometown of many a pirate, Bristol. Having played many notable roles on stage, television and in cinema, from playing Alan Bennett to Tony Hancock, from I, Claudius to Supernatural, and from The Spy Who Loved Me to perhaps his most well known role as Joshamee Gibbs in the Pirates of the Caribbean films.

Living in Chiswick with his wife, Phyllis, Kevin has recently completed his first novel, Sons of Sol, a science fiction comedy to be published in 2017.

Darrel Bevan: Colour-blind, Darrel is a portrait and figure illustrator who, due to colour blindness, specialises in graphite illustration—mainly on black and white images. When he isn't producing photorealistic pencil drawings, he teaches.

Guy Burtenshaw lives in a small town in southern England and has been writing horror stories for many years. He has self published several horror novels and a collection of short stories, and also writes murder mystery novels under the pseudonym G D Shaw.

Stephanie A. Craig is a Canadian speculative fiction writer. Her short story, "Jing Wei", appears in the Winter 2013 edition of *Mirror Dance Magazine* and *Luna Station Quarterly*, and she is currently working on her first novel. An avid sailor, she has had the fortune to avoid pirates, undead or otherwise, but probably only because she sails the Great Lakes. These do boast an impressive number of eels and supernatural serpents; however only if you look close enough. Stephanie studied classical literature and art at the University of Toronto. She lives in Port Credit with her husband, three daughters and a pugston. She can be found online at stephanieacraig. blogspot.ca

Alex Douglas-Mann works at an advertising agency in London's West End, though he is morally opposed to marketing as a whole. Before he got into advertising, he acted and performed stand-up comedy, but there was no money in it so he got a real job. He readily agrees that he is a sellout.

This bio was written from a tiny room in Brixton, where he lives with two cats that he has come to resent. When not brooding over what to do about the cats, he infrequently updates his website, www.fingerwords. com, where you can find more of his writing.

He is an Aquarius and knows how to sail, though neither of those facts have anything to do with him writing a story about a ship at sea. It's pure coincidence.

He has no other published works of note, and it's a sore point so don't ask him about it.

Stephanie Ellis is currently a Teaching Assistant in a Southampton secondary school but previously worked for many years as a technical author.

Her short stories, firmly based in the horror genre, have found success with a variety of publishers from magazine publications *Sanitarium* and *Massacre Magazine* to present and future anthology collections by

Fringeworks (including *Raus! Untoten!*, *Last Diner*, *Deadman's Tales* and *Cadaver*), Death Throes Publishing (*Distorted Perceptions*) and *100 Words or Less Horror Stories* by PopCorn Horror.

She also dabbles in poetry (printed in local and national press) and has recently distorted a number of favourite childhood nursery rhymes into something darker and more sinister, these can be found on her own website.

Her own taste in reading varies widely from Terry Pratchett, to Bernard Cornwell to current favourite Neil Gaiman—and oh yes, Stephen King and Edgar Allan Poe also get a look in.

Samples of her writing can be found on http://stephellis.weebly.com/, Readwave.com (where she is also a staff reviewer) and on 99Fiction.net. She can be found on twitter at @el_stevie.

Julius Horne (1906-2006) was a Staffordshire storyteller whose works went unpublished during his lifetime. A raconteur, a practising white magician, a collector of folk tales and other arcane stories, he claimed that many of his tales were drawn from real life, and that truth will always be stranger than fiction. He would have enjoyed the irony that his contribution is, quite literally, a dead man's tale.

Stewart Hotson has never escaped from pirates. Fortunately he's never been captured by them either. In fact, he lives in land, far from the sea and figures that this is a fool proof strategy for avoiding those scurvy types. Pleased with the surety of this plan he spends most days trying to solve other seemingly intractable problems like why flies land on the TV screen during tense moments in movies.

Kate Monroe is an author and editor who lives in a quiet and inspirational corner of southern England. She has penchants for chocolate, horror, and loud guitars, and a fatal weakness for red wine. Her interests in writing range from horror to erotica, taking in historical romance and tales of the paranormal on the way; whatever she has dreamed about the night before is liable to find its way onto the page in some form or another.

Her debut full-length novel, *The Falcon's Chase*, was released by Pink Pepper Press (an imprint of Sirens Call Publications) in 2012, and she has had short stories published in anthologies by Smart Rhino

Publications, Angelic Knight Press, Sirens Call Publications, Rainstorm Press, and Cruentus Libri Press. Her first horror novel, *Carpe Nectem*, was published in October 2013. Find more by visiting: @SerenKate and http://kateserenmonroe.com.

Patrick O'Neill is a rising talent in the world of Horror fiction. He resides in Dorset with beautiful wife, Nikki, and handsome son, Benedict. His dark and unsettling tales have featured alongside authors such as Jack Ketchum and Ramsey Campbell and can be found in the following publications: 'Alderway', in *Chiral Mad* by Written Backwards (Winner of the Compilations/Anthologies Category at the London Book Festival 2012). 'Passing Affliction' in *Chiral Mad 2, by Written Backwards*. 'Church Farm House' in *Fear: A Modern Anthology of Horror and Terror* by Crooked Cat. 'The Box' in *Dorset Voices* by Roving Press. 'The Collection' in *The Darkness Within* by Indigo Mosaic. 'The Westhoff Version' in *Darkness ad Infinitum* by Villipede Publications. 'Another Picture for the Wall' in *The Rogues Gallery* by Firbolg Publishing. 'The Setting Sea' in *The Sea Anthology* by Dark Continents Publishing. 'The Last Assignment' in *Voices from the Gloom Volume 2* by Siren's Call Publishing.

Patrick also writes under the pen-name *Benedict Ashforth* and has received high acclaim for his UK Amazon bestselling novella, *Abbot's Keep*. He can be contacted at padzoneill@hotmail.com

Rie Sheridan Rose's short stories appear in *Nightmare Stalkers and Dream Walkers vols 1 and 2, Cursed Curiosities, Come to My Window, Shifters, Reloaded: Both Barrels, These Vampires Don't Sparkle, The Grotesquerie* and *In the Bloodstream* as well as Yard Dog Press' *A Bubba In Time Saves None*. Yard Dog Press is also home to humorous horror chapbooks *Tales from the Home for Wayward Spirits and Bar-B-Que Grill* and *Bruce and Roxanne Save the World...Again*. Mocha Memoirs has "Drink My Soul...Please," and "Bloody Rain" as e-downloads. Online, she has appeared in *Cease, Cows,Lorelei Signal*, and *Four Star Stories*.

A.P. Sessler is a resident of North Carolina's Outer Banks and searches for that unique element that twists the commonplace into the weird. When he's not writing fiction, he composes music, dabbles in animation, and muses about theology and mind-hacking, all while watching way too many online movies.

His stories are most inspired by the works of Ray Bradbury, John Carpenter, the anthology films of Amicus Productions, and the occasional Italian horror film. His short stories have appeared in *Zippered Flesh 2*, *Dandelions of Mars*, *SQ Magazine*, and *Strangely Funny*.

A.P. lives in a small fishing village with his father, Luke, and their cat, Oreo.

K. R. Smith is an Information Technology Specialist and writer living in the Washington, D.C. area. While mainly interested in writing short horror stories, he occasionally delves into poetry, songwriting, and the visual arts. He recently had a poem, The Ballad of Drunken Jack, published in Gothic Blue Book III by Burial Day Books. Links to this and other works, including a myriad of flash fiction pieces, can be found on his blog at www.theworldofkrsmith.com. He may be reached via Twitter at @wokrsmith.

John Vicary began publishing poetry in the fifth grade and has been writing ever since. A contributor to many compendiums, his most recent credentials include short fiction in the collections "The Longest Hours", "Anthology of the Mad Ones" , "Midnight Circus" and issues of "Alternating Current", "Timeless Tales", and the Birmingham Arts Journal. He has stories in upcoming issues of Disturbed Digest, "Creepy Weird Horror Stories", "Plague: an Anthology of Sickness and Death" and a charity anthology entitled "Second Chance". John lives in rural Michigan with his family. You can read more of his work at keppiehed.com.

Max Wright is a corporate communications and occasional fiction writer living in the landlocked and largely pirate-free city of Dallas, Texas. His fantasy and horror stories have appeared in a number of magazines, e-zines and anthologies, and of course he's working on a novel. Or two. When he's not trying to scare people, he enjoys playing and officiating tennis, writers' group meetings, B-grade horror movies, military history and the pointless futility of being an ardent FC Dallas supporter. He'd also probably get more writing done if he wasn't so busy trying to keep up with two sons, two cats, a dog and a Craftsman home that's falling apart faster than he can repair it.

FIND OUT MORE ABOUT FRINGEWORKS BY USING THE QR CODE BELOW

OR VISIT
WWW.FRINGEWORKS.CO.UK

THANK YOU FOR READING

www.ingramcontent.com/pod-product-compliance
Lightning Source LLC
Chambersburg PA
CBHW030231180626
46810CB00008B/3072